Death in Deming

When 'Dangerous' Dan Tucker is asked to go to Deming, he looks on it as another routine case he doesn't want to do. He's forced to go there by Harvey Whitehill, US Marshal of Grant County, to help clean out a few bad men who have taken over the town for their own ends. His visit to the town is prompted by one need: money. He will do the job and retire from a life in which he knows he will end up dead. His suspicions about the town are confirmed when the murders begin.

Who is the man known as Wishart who does what he wants and avoids Tucker as much as he can? Why is he being threatened at every turn by forces he doesn't understand? Forced into a corner, Tucker does what he does best and comes out fighting. It's do-or-die time, and he isn't the one who is going to die.

Death in Deming

Alex Frew

A Black Horse Western

ROBERT HALE

© Alex Frew 2019
First published in Great Britain 2019

ISBN 978-0-7198-2886-7

The Crowood Press
The Stable Block
Crowood Lane
Ramsbury
Marlborough
Wiltshire SN8 2HR

www.bhwesterns.com

Robert Hale is an imprint
of The Crowood Press

Typeset by
Derek Doyle & Associates, Shaw Heath
Printed and bound in Great Britain by
4Bind Ltd, Stevenage, SG1 2XT

CHAPTER ONE

Marshal Harvey Whitehill, who was also a sheriff in his own jurisdiction of Grant County, looked at the man who was standing in front of him. The sheriff was seated in a bentwood chair behind the desk, a spot that was usually occupied by his companion. It was clear that this was no ordinary space, because alongside the marshal were eight cells. These were capable of holding twenty-four individuals at the most, although at three to a cell prisoners would find it rather cramped because these were by no means luxury abodes. It was perhaps a testament to the very people who were presently occupying the office space that all of those cells, bar none, were empty.

'So, I'll ask you again. Tucker,' said the marshal, shifting his long legs a little for comfort, 'will you do me just this one favour?'

'Harve, the favours you ask of me have a way of nearly getting me killed,' said his companion. Tucker was a man of medium height, and he was of such a bland appearance that it was hard to put a label to what he really looked like.

His features were pleasant and even, without being particularly remarkable in any way. Although he was far from what the ladies of Silver City, where they were currently ensconced, would have called 'handsome', he was far from ugly. Neither was he yet middle-aged, and indeed looked to be in his mid-thirties, while the marshal seemed older than his forty-odd years.

The two men contrasted in other ways too. Whitehill affected the long hair and the drooping moustache that had been common in the early days of Silver City, when it was just a tent city and barbers were in short supply. His hair was shot with streaks of grey that were not just there because of age, and his moustache was showing threads of silver. Tucker ran a hand through brown hair that was cut short, and he was clean-shaven. He was also neatly dressed in corduroy trousers, a dark green shirt and wore a black waistcoat. This was cut away in an unusual fashion at the hips, but anyone looking closely would have seen that this was because it would give him free access to the Colt .44 that sat holstered on either side. The last thing he needed was some minor entanglement that would prevent him from accessing the weapons as quickly as he wanted.

'Let me ask you something: what do you know about the town of Deming?' asked Whitehill, exhaling a cloud of smoke.

'Mighty little, to tell the truth, except that it's a spot where a garrison's worth of miners was headed in the last few months to try and find the alleged gold in the hills all around.'

'I think you're being a little disingenuous, my friend; there's something else about Deming that stands out.'

'What? You mean that railroad stuff? All that's happened is that the governor of this here territory of New Mexico took himself off, killed the fatted calf with the locals and drove a silver spike into a hole at the side of a metal rail.'

They both knew that this was a bold statement of fact that went a lot further than the words implied.

'Hell, if the meeting of the Southern Pacific with the Topeka Santa Fe railroads is a little event, I guess that description would do,' said Whitehill blandly. 'You do know that what happened that day just a little while ago, in this year of grace 1881, was the meeting of two huge railroads that go from "sea to shining sea", as stout Balboa might have said when he looked out at the Pacific.'

'There's money in that place,' said Tucker. 'I don't doubt that for a moment.'

'I met her, you know,' said Whitehill conversationally.

'What do you mean, "her"?'

'Mary Deming Crocker, the wife of Charles Crocker. Know who Charles Crocker is? He's one of the richest gents in America. He owns shares in both railroads. Well, he came through Silver City in 1877 with his wife on a fact-finding mission – no easy task, I can tell you. I became their personal escort out to what eventually became Deming. We had a few frightening moments, what with the weather and the injuns, but they were both determined to see what they were getting for his considerable investment. She was a wonderful lady, pretty and charming; you would have liked her.'

'Maybe so, but I don't see as to how it has any bearing on what you asked me to do.'

7

'Let's get straight down to it, Tucker. She was a gracious lady and I don't much like the idea of a town named after her being sullied by these miscreants.'

'What miscreants? That is the question.'

'That I don't rightly know,' said Whitehill, having the grace to look a little baffled. 'Deming, even though it's still under my jurisdiction, is making a lot of noises about splitting from Grant County and being within a jurisdiction called Luna. There's times when they don't seem to want my help at all, but the truth is the place is being overrun with those who would like to put it to their own use, take the money and run.'

'Excuse me for saying so, but why are you so bothered about a one-horse town that ain't known to most of the world? It's not as if they haven't got their own sheriff.'

'That's true, and when I helped get Mars appointed I though he was the right man. Now I'm not so sure.'

'Frank Mars?' Tucker looked genuinely interested for the first time. 'He was one of the defenders who went out with me during the salt wars. I even shared a tent with him out there. He was a good fighter when I thought we weren't going to survive the rebellion.'

'Then you'll go there for the sake of Frank?'

'It's still a no, Marshal,' said Tucker staunchly, ignoring the fact that the other man stood up for the first time, towering at least a head above his subordinate – a subordinate who was also a friend.

'You know the real reason I'm asking you to go, don't you?'

'I sure don't think it's out of real concern for the citizens of that little town, considering how you regard

Paschal.' Paschal was a nearby mining town beside Chloride Flats. There was some degree of enmity between the sheriff there, Gladius Moore, and the lawman that kept order in the mining camp, someone by the name of James Burns. They had a petty rivalry going on that was rooted in who had the right over the two territories when it came to enforcing justice, and Burns was very protective of what he saw as 'his' miners.

'Come to think of it,' said Tucker, 'why don't you send Moore? He likes to strut about as if he owns the place, maybe he'll settle their hash – whoever "they" are.'

'Gladius ain't the right man for the job, Dan, and you are,' said Whitehill. 'It's a pity Mayor Barkis is being so obstructive.' He thought about the matter for a minute. 'Just let me ask you, what do you think of Chicago?'

'I know they call it the city on the lake,' said Tucker. 'Haven't been yet; too busy running errands for a big smart-ass marshal.'

'You know what? In 1859, just before the Civil War, Chicago was mostly prairie land with hardly a building in sight. Just a few years later, at the end of the war it was a city of 80,000 people.'

'Well, Silver City's on the way to being that now.'

'I guess so, but then in 1871, just ten years ago, the city was scourged by fire. Did they let that bother them? No, sir; within a few days the new city was springing like a phoenix from the ashes of the old one. It now claims, with some reason, a population of half a million.'

'I don't see what this has to do with Deming.'

'That's the point, son. Chicago was made by the rail-road. Let me give you an example. When people come to

Chicago they come to the Grand Pacific Hotel, only a block away from the lake. I've been there. Do you know they have the most magnificent hall to be seen in the continental United States? They have the most wonderful apartments there, ones as good as those to be found in any city. You feel like a king in there.'

'Sounds good; I'll make a point of visiting,' said Tucker, with an air of indifference. He was an outdoor man, really. He had always been a rider of the plains.

'And the food, man, you've never seen the like; shad and whitefish from the eastern rivers, asparagus from Memphis, green peas from New Orleans, every fowl from duck to goose, roasted beef, and fruits of every variety – and that's just in one building.'

'I guess you like it there,' said Tucker.

'Twenty years ago that mighty city was wet and springy prairie; now the streets are paved with wooden blocks for the population to use in their daily perambulations. All right, it's taking a while for them to do it, but that's to be expected. The wooden blocks are being replaced with paving stones of fine granite, tall buildings are springing up wherever you go, the swamps that surrounded the city all overcome by progress.'

'Sounds like you ought to immigrate to Illinois right now.' The information still failed to excite Tucker. He would never be a city dweller.

'But that isn't the only reason Chicago is significant, not by a long way. In the early days, when she had a population of 80,000, she used to take in fifty thousand cattle. Now she receives over a *million*. In the early days she received two hundred thousand hogs. Now she receives over *four million.*'

'I think you're telling me this because it has something to do with Deming,' said Tucker, 'but at least it's stopped you from asking me to be your servant there.'

'They talk of other markets in the west, but Chicago has the biggest livestock markets to be found anywhere. The yards and buildings for the stock market cover hundreds of acres of land. They have hundreds of cattle yards, the same for hog and sheep pens, and their own network of water and sewer pipes. This is a huge operation never seen out here in the west before.'

'The point being?'

'Just be a little more patient with me, Tucker. Where was I? Oh yes, Chicago receives cattle from Missouri, the upper Mississippi, Nebraska, Kansas, Wyoming, Dakota, Colorado, the distant plains of the Texas Rio Grande and, of course, from right here in New Mexico.'

'Sounds like a mighty big operation to me, and one they'll never equal anywhere else. Not around here, at least,' said Tucker, but there was a little twist to his smile as he spoke that showed he knew exactly what he was saying.

'That's clearly the point,' said the marshal. 'With the meeting of two transcontinental railroads, there's no reason why Deming can't be developed in the same way as Chicago. The southwest could become a centre of industry of the cattle business. Think of it: we're not that far from the Mexican border. We could trade with that very country instead of engaging in countless wars, driving through millions of heads of cattle a year as the population of the area expands.' Tucker could not help noting that there was a shining look to the marshal's expression

11

that seemed oddly out of kilter when compared his normal poker face. This was a man who had a mission very close to his heart. They talked about evangelicals, and that all that stuff was connected with God, whoever that might be, but people could have a mission close to their hearts that gave them just as much zeal as any religion.

'You don't even know the half of it, Tucker. The railroad company has built a huge hotel in Deming called the Metrople. It's nothing compared to the Grand Pacific, but it's a huge investment, and think of the reason why. The amount of travellers coming to this area is set to rise by the hundreds of thousands every year. And there's a possibility it might all turn to ashes.'

'Let's see: you're putting so much weight on my shoulders that if I don't do this I'm destroying the chances of Deming becoming a city? Thanks, Harve.'

'I'm going to ask you this directly, Tucker: will you please take on this last job and then you can get on with your life?' By the time the words were out of his mouth, Tucker was already heading for the front door with the air of a man who has a great deal to achieve and needs to get on with his day.

'Just because it's you, I'll think about it,' said Tucker with a pleasant nod, closing the door behind him on the way out. 'But think about it is all I'm doing,' he said *sotto voce* as he climbed down the steps leading up to the office.

CHAPTER TWO

Silver City was exactly what it pretended to be: an ever-growing town founded on the premise that there was an inexhaustible supply of silver to be found in the district. Tucker knew that as early as 1833 Kit Carson had travelled across the plains with a band of Crow Indians, and that the intrepid explorer had named the surrounding area Gold Canyon where he panned in the sluggish waters of the river for gold, finding enough to give rise to the name. The surrounding hills, troughs and the descents beneath gave rise to what was the real discovery in the area – that the earth contained possibly millions of tons of silver ore.

This was not a process that had happened overnight. Geologists had come out and assessed the potential of the area in the '50s, pronouncing on the huge reserves of silver lying locked into the ground. At the tail end of the Civil War a great deal of time and investment was put into the area, with Uncle Sam encouraging investment companies to bring men here and set up production facilities. The systematic search for metal had started, while other settlers came in and looked for gold rather than silver because it was more profitable and easier to get in some ways, through near-surface digging and the panning of waters.

These lone prospectors worked at claims that were managed carefully by a licensing office in the town. When Harve Whitehill arrived there from Ohio in 1871, appointed and charged with being the representative of the forces of law and order in this county, much of his work had to do with disputes over claims, claim jumpers, and the violent and frequently bloody feuds that often occurred over such events.

Whitehill was no softhearted fool; he had hung quite a few men in the court of rough justice in his day, showing the rest what their fate would be if they behaved badly. He was a God-fearing, upright man who rarely drank, while in his personal life he was somewhat staid but faithful to his principles, which meant that he gained a great deal of respect and trust in the community.

Tucker unhitched his horse and made his way through the streets of Silver City. From humble beginnings, when it was little more than a succession of tents and mud-brick dwellings, the city had acquired a solidly built Main Street where many of the shop-fronts and the goods within would not have disgraced a large city like Houston or New York – another sign of the changes wrought by the rail-roads.

As Tucker rode towards the outskirts of town the more solidly-built dwellings gave way to low-frame houses that were a throwback to the early days, with many barely more than elaborate tents hastily put together and shored up with whatever available materials were at hand.

14

The quartz mills were on the outside of the town, separated from it by a series of railroad switches and yards containing long, low buildings with timber walls and corrugated iron roofs. These buildings were known as sheds. The mills themselves were made of a more solid grey brick that housed the machinery within.

A pallid smoke lay over the whole area, the smell of which contained an acrid tinge so that if some drifted his way, which it often did, it would make Tucker cough if he breathed it in, and the acidity would make his eyes water.

As he rode he tried not to think of those who toiled below him, often hundreds of feet below the earth. He could not imagine living such a life, yet there were thousands of men in Grant County who turned into human moles and spent their youth – for most of them were young – toiling in earth, mud, mire and darkness for a few grains of precious metal.

Not far from the quartz mills were the cones of crushed stone that had been worked over and discarded. These raised high above the sheds and dominated the skyline like silent giants who were just biding their time, waiting to stir.

Silver City was based on a series of terraces that rose into the hills, with the meanest dwellings above and the best below in stark contrast to most cities of that type, where those with the most money would establish grand homes in the hills. There was another reason for this: most of the mining owners did not live out here, but back east.

Tucker rode out of the valley, which rose and fell like undulating waves, until he was high enough, once over the bluff of a hill, to see his ranch, a sight that gladdened his

15

eyes. The Bar-Q had been purchased by Tucker from a rancher whose sons had decided that they were going to make their fortunes in other trades. Old Man Ryan, the rancher, had decided that he wanted to retire to a larger city – in this case out east – and find a woman to share his ease, his wife having passed away more than twenty years since.

Even out here he could still hear the distant but muffled clunking of the mills as he rode towards his spread, and he noted that his arrival had been observed; his farm manager, Taylor, was coming out to see him.

Josh Taylor was a big, solid man who, as he came forward on his big roan, stopped the progress of his employer before he could get much further. The ranch was behind him. It was a good size, taking in a great deal of land, most of it being unfenced except for the area around the main building, the barn and all the smaller outbuildings such as the tack room and the stables that were needed in an operation of this size. The pastures, too, were fenced with a windmill at each side of the farm tapping into the aquifers that flowed far beneath the soil of the land and brought up the precious water that kept the grass green so that he could feed his herd.

Side by side, leading their horses, the two men walked the remaining distance leading to the ranch. Taylor was dressed in stout boots and blue overalls beneath which he wore a somewhat grey cotton shirt. Dressed in this way, with his balding head and his rural method of speaking, he looked like a slow, solid workman. He was the kind of man who might toil for ten hours in a row without having much more on his mind than a beer and a steak at the end

16

of the day.

Like all men who have to make acute judgements in their daily life, Tucker was not fooled by this apparent density of being. Taylor had been a foreman in the mines, and he was a shrewd man with an aptitude for planning ahead that went well with the job of manager. In the spring he would be anticipating what would happen come the winter months, he would plan for contingencies such as feed shortages due to drought, and on the opposite scale what would happen when the monsoon rains came pouring down. He was also not a man to shirk from his duty.

'You haven't been here for a few weeks, Dan. I've kept the news from you because I wanted to tell you in person.'

'What news?'

'Your new herd has cattle cough.'

'I know that. They were brought in by rail; you know what happens to animals travelling in carriages in those conditions. The dust gets into 'em from the sand and dust in the cattle trucks. It should start clearing up any day now.'

'Dan, that's why I waited.' They both remembered the day the herd was brought in from the nearby (comparatively speaking) railroad. They were solid beeves, not like the Longhorns that were traditionally bred out here, but big black-and-white Durhams with horns that sprouted upwards for only a few inches. They were amiable animals that had a reputation for being good for both milk and meat – products that would find a ready market in town, where there was an insatiable appetite for such things.

Even then he had noticed there was a certain degree of

17

wetness about their mouths and nostrils, and some laboured breathing amongst some of the individuals, but then he had been assured by the cattle agent, one James Pike, that the dust from their journey had affected them adversely and that any problems in that regard would soon settle down. Pike was the same agent who had departed soon afterwards with his money, never to be seen again.

'So it ain't a dust cough?' asked Tucker.

'The truth is, it looks like a regular cattle cough to me,' said Taylor, 'the one caused by infection.' Although Tucker had not been a cattle man before making what now looked like an ill-advised purchase, he had seen enough information to know about the dreaded infection. It was similar to pneumonia and tuberculosis in humans in that it was caused by bacteria that got into the lungs. People gave the animals their own infusions made of thinned-out molasses and alcohol, but in fact there was very little that could be done once a herd was affected except to hope that it would pass.

'Let's have a look at them,' said Tucker, the first thing any wise man would do. They hitched their horses and went to where the herd was penned up in a roomy pasture behind the ranch. With only an occasional bellow the beasts looked at him with dull eyes and heaving chests. Most of them had lost weight since he had last seen them.

'Why didn't you get in touch with me sooner?' he asked.

'I sent messages for you to come, but I guess you were engaged elsewhere,' said Taylor.

Tucker did not argue with him. As the sheriff of these parts he had been given an engagement that went well above the call of duty. Two robbers – their names didn't matter – had robbed the takings of one of the big hotels in Silver City. Tucker had been at a loss to find them because they gone off into the hills, but a couple of days later a smallholder called Norrie Stevens had wandered into town complaining that some rather angry gents had turned him out of his own dwelling in a nearby valley. They would have killed him too if it had not been for the fact that he had been working outside when they had raided the area. Norrie had run for his life with bullets zinging past his ears, and it was only by sheer luck that he had survived long enough to get into town.

Tucker could have easily been caught up in a gunfight, which would have involved recruiting some of the local men as his posse, riding out to the valley and bearding the outlaws in their den. He was, however, not made of that kind of stuff.

The outlaws would be certain that the smallholder had perished in the desert. Tucker simply took a couple of horses, weapons and enough food for a couple of days and headed for the valley in question. He also got Norrie, the smallholder, to accompany him, and this might have been risky since the older man had been through so many privations lately. But this was not a sudden confrontation; that was not Tucker's way. Instead he took shelter in a rocky enclave to which he was guided by his companion, who knew the landscape better than anyone else since it was around here he made his living, and then Tucker simply kept an eye on the building in the valley. It was a far from palatial place in which to live; it was really just a temporary hidey-hole, and within another day the two outlaws came out and started making preparations to get away with their ill-gained loot.

The building was a short distance away from a jumble of boulders, some taller than a man. Tucker stepped out from these and asked in a forthright manner for the two men to surrender and they would be taken to jail and given a fair trial. They had reacted immediately by pulling out their guns and starting to shoot at him. They were shooting from light into shade, and the harshness of the sun on their heads meant that they were shooting at the most vague of shadows. Tucker, who had thought the matter out, was shooting from shade into light, which meant that his targets were superbly illuminated. Also, the landowner was with him, a man who stepped out and used a shotgun to help Tucker complete the job.

Less than a minute after the shouted warning and the invitation to comply with the law, the two raiders were laying dead, one with a hole in the heart and the other with a head full of lead.

Tucker had arrived back in Silver City alone, with a saddlebag full of money. The owner of the hotel had already told him the amount – five thousand dollars – and every penny was there.

As for those who had committed the crime, strictly speaking he should have brought in their bodies and filled in the necessary paperwork, but by a sort of tacit agreement, and with the help of the smallholder, he had buried the bodies at the outer edge of the property. Nobody had been killed in the raid on the hotel, which would have made matters a lot more awkward, and the owner was quite happy to get his money back and let the matter rest there.

Along with this event, and others that had taken him away from his investment, Tucker always had it in the back of his mind that he was going to retire from the law and get away from a life in which the odds were that an unlucky bullet would come his way at some point and take off the top of his head.

Now his prospects were lying in ruins.

'Once this gets out, I'll be finished,' he said. 'I'll have no credence whatsoever as a rancher.' He swallowed hard. He was the kind of man who would face up to consequences. 'Have them slaughtered as quickly as you can. Is there anything we can save?'

'I guess we could tan their hides and the bones could go for glue,' said Taylor, 'but the meat will be useless; it won't pass inspection.'

'Then I'm done for,' said Tucker, feeling the one thing he had never known before in his professional life: a kind of numb despair. 'I should have been here sooner.'

'There wasn't much you could do,' said Taylor, 'if that's any comfort to you.'

'I could have been tracking down that weasel of a dealer,' said Tucker. 'Had some of my money back but he's well away now.' His face hardened as he said this and it was obvious that if he had another encounter with Mr Pike then the event would not end well for one of them.

'There's a way of dealing with this,' said Taylor.

'How? I'm finished now.'

'I can employ labourers heading for Mexico,' said Taylor. 'Men come over every year and work in the mines then go back to their own country. I can soon muster five or six, get the job done quickly, pay them and they'll head

21

off where they have to go. Most of 'em don't speak English that well anyway, so you'll be able to keep your secret that way.'

In his own way Tucker was touched by the concern being shown for him by his manager.

'Josh, that would be great, except for one little thing: I put most of my money into this venture. I can't afford to pay your wages, or Kathy's for that matter.' Kathy, Taylor's wife, was the housekeeper for the ranch, a large, motherly woman who always made Tucker feel as if he was the centre of the world.

'Don't worry about that,' said Taylor stoutly. 'We'll hang on as long as we can.' He did not remind Tucker that he, Taylor, owned a property in Silver City that he rented out. It was a form of savings that meant he and his wife were not solely dependent on the income they made from working at the ranch.

'I'll see what I can do from my end,' said Tucker, 'but you'll make the arrangements for me?'

'Trust me,' said Taylor, 'I'll get this done and not a word'll get out.'

'Why are you doing this for me?' asked Tucker bluntly. 'I thought you would have run off at the first chance.'

'It ain't going to be the greatest event in my life,' said Taylor, 'but before I came to you I worked the mines.' A haunted look came into his eyes. 'You've got no idea what it was like to be down there, in the darkness, the heat. Even as a supervisor it was hard going, and I ain't afraid of hard work, but there's a reason why it's young men down there.' He said no more, but Tucker got the message.

22

CHAPTER THREE

In his own mind Tucker drew a veil over the events of the next few days. He was not a man who suffered a great deal from conscience, since the deeds he had committed in the past had always come from a place where he had felt that he was in the right. There was nothing right about this situation, and no one was a winner in the end, but he could rest secure in the knowledge that the animals he had taken into his care were no longer suffering, and that was some small comfort, although not much when he contemplated the entire situation.

He worked with Taylor and the promised band of men, who did their job with an efficiency borne from being driven by supervisors in the mines, and who left for the Mexican border afterwards. He was satisfied that he would never see them again. Once they went back most of them would never return and, even if they did, they had very little English between them and the task they had completed was just another job, albeit a harsh one. His secret was safe for the time being.

In the meantime, with what little he had left, he paid off

the men and gave wages to his manager, and also what was almost his last sum of money: a couple of hundred dollars.

'Go out,' he said to Taylor, 'and buy in a few beeves. Just say you're always expanding the market. But before you do, make sure the open areas and the grids are washed down with disinfecting fluid to get rid of any traces of the disease.'

Taylor looked as if he was going to protest at this, mainly because he knew how close Tucker was to financial ruin, and then he closed his mouth again. As far as he was concerned, Tucker might have made a big mistake – and every man had a right to one of those in his life – but in general the sheriff knew what he was doing.

'I have to leave now,' said Tucker, a few days after their earlier conversation when he had helped them complete their self-imposed but awful task.

He went back to Silver City. When he had ridden away from the city he had been looking at the prospect of leaving forever, or at least returning for the purpose of carrying out one or two arrests, demoting his own status to that of a deputy who would be called upon to help out when he was needed. Now he was returning for the purpose of simply earning money.

In the back of his head there was an idea that was half-formed about robbing a local business or one of the three banks that had sprung up in the town. If you mixed with outlaws long enough you sometimes began to think like them. He had the knowledge he needed to carry out such an act, because as the sheriff he had inspected most of the local businesses to consult with them on how good their security arrangements were. It was an act he could probably get away with, would provide the funds for the immediate survival of his ranch, and stop his ruin.

The thought was one that did not last for long. The truth was he might be able to get away with such an act and never get caught, but he would never be able to live with himself, and would surely retreat to the bottle to get away from the bad dreams. That was enough to make him dismiss the idea out of hand.

When he got back to his office – after all the fuss he had made that he had needed the time off – he almost sighed with relief. The office was in a big, roomy building that had been created with funds from the grateful citizens of the town who had voted almost unanimously for some kind of law and order – the exception being those who wanted law and order to simply disappear. Besides the eight cells, and a big, roomy office illuminated by two large windows set in the walls behind his desk, with other, smaller windows to the side; the office was attached to living quarters.

The accommodation was far from fancy, but it had several rooms, one of which was a small cubby-hole where he could do his own private paperwork, while there was a kitchen area with a stove that could be fired up and provide the means to make hot meals and keep the place heated at night.

He was weary and the jail was empty, so he went into his quarters and lay down on the narrow bed. He could see now that work was often a solace for men, a way of getting away from the troublesome world and back to a simpler existence. Taylor, for instance, would fight tooth and nail to keep the ranch going because he did not want to lose a way of life that, whatever its drawbacks, had freed him from a hellish existence underground.

For the first time in several days he began drifting off into a natural sleep untroubled by bad dreams. He awoke to hear the sound of voices, swung his feet over the side of the bed and drew on his boots.

The one thing he had recognized immediately was that the voices were familiar, and as he stood in the doorway that led from his quarters to the office he could see Harvey Whitehill sitting behind the desk in that familiar pose, addressing the new arrival who stood in front of him.

The man being addressed was young, with a shock of dark hair and a holstered gun on his right hip. Without hearing his voice, Tucker would have immediately recognized the new arrival as Gladius Moore. Whitehill had waited for the return of his sheriff friend, and when this had not happened he had taken up Tucker's own suggestion.

'Howdy,' said that individual from the doorway. Moore turned immediately, reaching at the gun on his hip from pure instinct, a move which Tucker reciprocated, but they both relaxed as the newcomer was recognized and they nodded to each other.

'Hello there, my old friend Glad,' said Tucker.

'Dan, I thought you were gone for a little while,' said Harvey. 'I don't think the fire-irons are all that necessary, do you?'

Moore came into the room and stood a short distance from his fellow sheriff, a man who was not exactly a friend. The look on Gladius' face was one of pure annoyance. He was a man in his late twenties and still had the eager expression of one who has not been beaten down by life.

'Good thing for you I know you,' he said. He was dressed in clean, dark trousers, had long boots and wore a red shirt atop of which was a dark green waistcoat with gold-plated buttons. He wore his six-pointed county badge in a prominent manner, high up on his lapel; because he had to stoop a little to look the likes of Tucker in the face, that meant that people's faces saw the badge all the time. He was also, as Tucker knew, a bit of a heartbreaker; his good looks and easy manner had a way of sweeping the ladies off their feet.

'Why is it a good thing?' asked Tucker mildly.

'Because if you had been a stranger you could have got the top of your blamed head blown off.'

'"Could" being the instrumental word, friend.' Tucker spoke mildly, but this only seemed to incense Moore a little, the sheriff of Paschal being a man who was quick to perceive an insult in even the most innocuous remark.

'I say *would* then,' he replied.

'No point continuing down that track, you two officers,' interrupted Whitehill, who by this time was standing close to them getting ready to intervene. 'I've brought Gladius here to see if he's interested in that little job I was mentioning to you a few days ago.'

'It depends,' said Moore, 'if it won't take long. I have a situation brewing in my own town with James Burns, and it won't remain under cover for long.' He spoke the name of Burns with the kind of contempt normally reserved for discussing the Red Indians and their ways.

'That's funny, because I came here to discuss the very same thing – the Deming affair,' said Tucker calmly, even

27

though he suddenly saw a source of useful income being snatched from his grasp.

'Sorry, Tucker, you had your chance. It's time for a new boy to take on the task.'

'I've been away. I've had a few days rest; now I'm ready to do as you ask.'

'Rest?' said Moore contemptuously. 'You look done in, man, there are bags beneath your eyes I could pack and take on holiday, and your cheeks are hollow. You look done in.'

'Well, I'm not.' Tucker did not show his feelings on the surface. He had always been that way, but he was getting angry with his fellow sheriff. 'Let me do this, Harvey. I won't let you down.'

Whitehill did not say anything for a while. He was clearly weighing one man against the other and considering the possible cost of choosing Moore over Tucker. When he finally spoke it was in a light but friendly manner, in an attempt to gloss over the situation.

'Gladius, I guess I might have brought you out here on a fool's errand,' said Whitehill, 'but if Tucker's manning up to the task he really is the best man for the job.'

'The hell you say?' There was a cold expression on Moore's face. 'So this little pipsqueak appears and I get shoved out?' The truth was he did not really want to go all the way to Deming. As far as he was concerned, Whitehill had been calling in a favour, but he wasn't about to let this fact interfere with his genuine annoyance at being usurped by a newcomer.

'You'll be paid for your time,' said Whitehill. 'Thanks for coming along. Stick around and we'll all go for a drink when this is settled.'

'No drinks for me. I'm going back to Paschal,' said Moore stiffly. 'Go suck in with your pet sheriff, Harve. Goodbye.' He ignored the presence of Tucker and went out, rattling the door in its frame in a manner that indicated he was not best pleased with the marshal's decision.

'What brought you back?' asked Whitehill. For a moment Tucker was tempted to tell him everything, to confide in the man who had given him the chance to do the deeds that had given him enough money to buy the ranch in the first place. But it was not his nature to share his feelings.

'Money,' he said, surprised at the coldness of his tone. 'Money, and plenty of it, too. If things are as bad in Deming as you say then I'm at a risk to life and limb. That kind of assignment doesn't come cheap.'

'How much?'

'I want five thousand dollars,' said Tucker, 'with a thousand as a deposit right now.' At a time when a deputy earned a couple of thousand a year, that was a lot of money. Whitehill's eyebrows shot up and vanished into his long fringe.

'You ask a helluva lot.'

'Really? Well, get together a posse of your best men and go into Deming and sort it out that way, or send in Moore and let him blast away at every danged object he sees.' They both knew that Whitehill must have been desperate indeed if he had been considering using Moore.

'Look, I can't go with a troop – although I might have to do so if this doesn't get sorted soon,' said Whitehill. 'I'll be blunt; these things get in the papers. This is a brand new town, financed by the railroads, with hopes that it will become a new city for this territory. If I went in with my men and blasted the area, what kind of message would that send?'

'It would send a message that here was a man who wasn't going to be messed with.'

'Mebbe so, but it would also make big headlines that I don't need.' Whitehill squinted at the figures he had scribbled on the yellow pad in front of him. He was in the habit of scribbling thus when deep in thought, and the pad was covered in little doodles. 'How you arrived at the money is beyond me, but I guess I have pushed you lately. A mess arises and you clean it up. I'll get you three thousand dollars.'

'Guess I'll just have to say no, then,' said Tucker with that quiet stubbornness for which he was famous. Whitehill had another quick think about the matter. 'All right, five thousand then.'

'With the deposit up front.'

'You'll get your deposit.'

There was a strained silence between the two, then they sat down to smoke, relax and discuss the matter in more detail, and even though this was a lifestyle he had rejected, Tucker felt as if he was slipping into a warm, comfortable bath, albeit one that might have piranhas lurking just below the surface.

He was at home.

CHAPTER FOUR

Frank Mars sat on one of the comfortable green-painted benches on platform two of Deming railroad station. He was acutely aware of his surroundings. The line had been finished just a few months ago and the governor of New Mexico had driven in a silver spike to commemorate the joining of the Atchison, Topeka and Santa Fe (ATSF) from the east with the Southern Pacific from the west. Deming, as the spot where the two lines were joined, was not just considered to be an important town on the route; it was the one that was considered to be the one with the most potential. This had been driven home to him and made him nervous.

The railroad station was far from just being a place where passengers could alight and spend some time before going elsewhere; it was a wide, roomy building, several storeys high and it had a steep roof and deep eaves that left the platforms in shadow so that they would have to be lit by oil lamps at night. This might have seemed a strange thing to do, but it was because during the heat of the day the stony platforms could become unbearably hot, and by bringing a projecting roof over the platforms this gave passengers a welcome shade in which to shelter from the heat of the heavenly orb.

Frank Mars was younger than Tucker and so thin that the loose jacket he wore and his long, black trousers seemed to envelop his body. He held his naturally thin body in a very upright manner, and his jaw had a determined set to it that did not seem to auger well for whoever he was going to be dealing with. Neither did the shotgun lying across his lap. He might have been a good-looking young man if it had not been for the set look on his face.

The steam train Belle of the South came trailing into the station with several Pullman cars being pulled behind. The noise of the train coming to a halt and the amount of steam that poured out of the funnel meant that, for a couple of minutes, he could see nothing of the passengers. Besides, the platform was already busy; several porters were already making their way up its length to assist the passengers with their luggage. Then a guard carrying a red flag and a whistle alighted from the train, opening the doors briskly as he walked along the platform and signalling with his whistle as he did so.

A stolid-looking man emerged from one of the carriages pulling out a large leather trunk, which he deposited on one of the platform trolleys, waiting there for such an event to happen. He had a brief word with one of the porters, a gent who called him 'sah'. and seemed intent on taking the trolley from him, but the new arrival was having nothing to do with this and pulled the vehicle behind him as he trundled down the platform.

It was the turn of Mars to stand up and come forward, the set look still on his face.

'Frank Mars, well, well,' said the new arrival, and held out a hand. Mars transferred the shotgun to his other hand and faced the man who had looked after him in his youth, and shook hands in a perfunctory manner.

'What the hell are you doing here?' he asked.

'Frank, you look as if you need a good feed,' said Tucker. 'Mind, you was always a skinny lad, especially when you were nineteen or so.'

'This ain't a gab fest between two pals,' said Mars with a degree of heat in his tone. 'I got word, I guess because Whitehill was obliged to let me know you were on your way.'

'I guess,' said Tucker mildly. 'Good of you to come out and get me, because I'd have been obliged to look you up.'

'You ain't going to answer me, fine,' said Mars, 'but how's about I put it this way: what do you say you get on the next train heading in the opposite direction and stay on?' Tucker, though, was not a man for direct confrontation unless it was due. He seemed to be all set on pretending that they were taking up the friendship where it had left off.

'There's a sign up there. Looks like we can go in and get a coffee for less than 50 cents each. Trying to attract the customers, eh?' He steered them towards the coffee shop, ignoring anything else implied in the stance of his former friend. There was a coffee shop, as he had so acutely observed at the station side, facing the platform onto which he had just emerged. The surround was green and the shutters were painted white. The unmistakeable scent of coffee and warm rolls from inside was like pollen to a bee for Tucker. The café even had small tables on the outside, mimicking the Parisian street scenes in a painting by Degas.

Tucker ordered coffee and a couple of rolls and cooked ham, while his companion declined anything to eat but accepted a coffee. Living up to his name, Tucker tucked into what was really his breakfast. He had set off while it was still dark and it was still early in the morning.

'I needed that,' he said with some degree of satisfaction as he lit a cigarette and smoked thoughtfully in between taking long draughts of his coffee. He had ordered a full pot, so there was plenty to go round.

Just along the platform, another man had appeared when the passengers were getting off the train and the steam was blowing about. Mars, intent on his prey, had not seen him arrive, but the new arrival had looked at the bearing of Sheriff Tucker, and he had seen Mars shaking hands with him. As if a suspicion had been confirmed, he turned away and left the station, like someone who is bearing bad news, just before the two men went for their coffee.

'I remember how we became good buddies,' said Tucker. 'Long time ago now.'

'The San Elizario Salt Wars,' said Mars with a degree of pride. It was the first time he had thawed since their meeting. Old memories have a way of doing that to an individual.

'Thing is,' said Tucker, 'insurrection is a terrible thing, what with the Mexican Wars having taken place

34

just before the Civil War. If it had been allowed to continue it could have led to a war between Texas and
Mexico.'

The two of them had fought side by side against that
particular peasant uprising. He had saved Mars' life once
or twice, but Mars had repaid the favour at least once.
They both relaxed while talking about the Salt Wars.

This time round, though, Mars seemed nervous, in
that there was indifference about him, and a defiant attitude. Tucker knew where this came from. At nineteen,
Mars had been a mere youth who was willing to defer to
one whom he saw as superior; now he was taking the attitude that this was his town and Tucker was an intruder.
The moment of amity between them began to slip away as
Tucker stood up and grasped the handle of the platform
trolley.

'Well, it's been might good to see you again, Frank. I
only hope we'll be able to work together on this one.
You're the man who should have a grasp of what's going
on.'

'So you're not leaving despite what I've said?'

'I've been sent here by a higher power, and I don't
mean God,' said Tucker, 'although I am on a mission.' For
a moment the amiable exterior vanished and his normally
placid face took on a sharper, leaner aspect, as if the real
man within was peeking through a veiled curtain. 'I ain't
here to mess around, Frank. Once I get this stuff settled in,
you and me, we're going to meet in your office and we're
going to have a real good discussion. Oh, and I'll be
staying right here. I see this is more than a railroad station.
A hotel too, who'd have believed it?' He was soon out of

35

sight and Mars sat where he was for a moment. He finished his coffee with a thoughtful look on his face, then got up and loped out of the railroad station.

CHAPTER FIVE

William Wishart looked out of the second floor window of the Metrople over the town that was now his and felt gratified at the sight. Business was booming, and his business was money. Wishart was a big man in his early thirties who looked as if he might have seen rougher days. This was plain to see on features that were lined beyond his years. He had come from Colorado at a time when people were going there to look for gold – a fool's journey, he believed. In his mind he tried to suppress the fact that he himself, in his twenties, had been one of the fools.

He moved in a way that contrasted a great deal with his size. People who saw his solid frame and how wide he was in the shoulders often mistook him for a slow-moving man, but he could proceed with lightning speed when he wanted. This fact had saved his life in the mining town of Telluride more than once, especially where jealous husbands were involved. This morning he was having a treat. The hipbath was sitting there on an oval rug away from the window. Two large white towels on the bed testified to the end point of the luxury act. There was a screen behind which he could get changed if he so desired. The bath was already partly filled with steaming water and, as he stood there in his long johns, there was another rap on the door to follow the several he had already heard that morning.

'Come in,' he said, moving away from the window and sitting on the bed. The door opened and a maid entered carrying two large ceramic ewers filled to the brim with boiling water.

'What are you doing, sir?' she asked, for it was understood that he would remain discreetly out of sight while his bath was being prepared.

'Waiting,' said Wishart. 'Especially for a pretty little thing like you.' The maid ignored him; the truth was that she matched his description, for she was barely out of her teenage years and had curves in all the right places, while her face, which at this moment was expressing distaste at encountering a partially clothed man (in her eyes he was obviously no gentleman) had a mouth that was only too kissable and a pair of the bluest eyes he had ever seen. She ran the water into the bath with an air that said she would have preferred to dump it over the occupant of the room.

'I see you're busy,' said Wishart, coming towards the young woman. 'Are you too busy for all things?' As he came forward she turned, and he was so close that one of the ewers caught the back of the hand that he was raising to reach out and touch her. He gave a sharp gasp of pain and pulled back because the ceramic hide of the jug was still extremely hot, like one of the similarly ceramic hot water bottles used to warm the beds for patrons on request.

'Oh, I'm sorry, sir,' said the girl, withdrawing neatly

38

from him as she set down one of the jugs and pulled his room door open. 'I'll get you some cold water now to put in to suit yourself.' She glanced back at him; the expression on his face was like thunder. 'Although why you can't use one of our fancy new bathrooms, I don't know. That's what they're for.'

'What's your name?' asked Wishart.

'Kathleen,' she said, flashing those blue eyes at him, 'my friends call me Kathy. You can call me Kathleen.'

'There's a lot of sass in you,' he said. 'I ought to report you to management.'

'I *am* management,' she said, 'my father runs this establishment. I was away for a while, and now I'm back I'm helping out because there's been a fresh load of guests and one of the girls is sick.'

'Well, perhaps you can come to a little arrangement with me,' Wishart smiled and showed teeth as crooked as the gravestones in a neglected churchyard. 'What say I get in this thing, you give me five minutes to get sudsed up, and come and scrub my back? You see, the reason for this here is that I like the personal service, and your service comes trudging to me, not the other way about.' He could also have added that he was slightly intimidated by the shiny new bathroom on the ground floor. Being financed by the railroads, the Metrople had provided the best for new arrivals, but Wishart wasn't used to that kind of luxury.

'I'll scrub you,' she said, 'with a club on the back of the head if you come near me again, Mr Wishart.' With that she picked up her magnificent jugs and moved briskly out of the room and the door, which, being on springs like most in the hotel, slammed behind her.

The promised cold water was brought to him by a different girl, who seemed to have been forewarned that their visitor was a little frisky, because she put the ewers of cool liquid just inside the door and left immediately. Wishart frowned a little. He was in a position of power; he could go out and meet a woman who could give him what he wanted – this was his town, after all – but he couldn't help pondering on the beauty of the manager's daughter. He had his bath, singing to himself as he did so, and dried with the towels that had been laid out by the same beautiful lady who had wounded him. The scald she had given him had smarted for a little while.

Wishart dressed in the clothes that had been laid out for him. He put on a white collared shirt, a canvas double-breasted vest and a pair of trousers, the background of which was a dark gold but with narrow and wider red stripes atop. These were held up under his vest by a pair of black elastic braces. Over his dark cotton socks he pulled a pair of tan brogan boots made of fine, soft leather.

Still thinking of Kathleen, he completed the assembly by donning his frock coat, which was a very dark green with a herringbone pattern. He completed this outfit by sliding a Prince Edward gold watch, attached by a lapel chain, into his waistcoat pocket, and donned a John Bull top hat with a shine that had been put there by another servant the previous night.

With this assemblage completed he stepped down to the main body of the hotel. He met Kathleen on the way down and swept off his hat to her.

'My dear, do forgive me for my temporary lapse. Please

40

see your way to dining with me later in this very establishment. I am sure your father will not object.' He could see from the quirk in her bowed lips that she was in a mood to refuse, and hastily added an addendum to his words. 'I am spending a great deal of money here; your father might be displeased if you were not to please your guests, and a meal is nothing.'

'Very well, Mr Wishart, a meal it shall be and nothing else. More help has arrived to carry out my duties so I shall be free. Lunch only.' She was carrying an armful of towels for the guests and hurried onwards while he looked back and admired her firm, youthful frame. He had known the threat of withdrawing business would have that effect on her, good as he was at manipulating his surroundings.

Like all of his other acts he would be found out and confronted sooner or later, but by that time he hoped to have wielded enough power to become a very rich man indeed.

He was outside the hotel for what was disguised as his morning stroll – really a business trip to make sure that everything was still being done his way and under wraps – when a dark-faced youth came rapidly towards him. The young man was dressed as a cowboy and had a look of disdain on his features similar to that of Kathleen, but this time not aimed at Wishart.

'Ruiz Montero,' said Wishart, but not too loudly, 'I do not really need to see you right now.'

'I think you do,' said Montero.

The two stopped and conversed briefly. To a passing stranger it would have looked as if a gentleman gambler was being accosted for money by a penniless cowboy, and

41

their exchange was soon done with and Wishart strolled on without looking back. This time the expression on his somewhat rugged features, that were so out of step with the clothing he wore, was one of serious thought that boded ill for whomever Ruiz had been discussing with him.

CHAPTER SIX

Tucker was given a room on the ground floor at the front of the building. The room was tastefully appointed in cream and green with a carpeted floor and a brand new bed. In fact, everything was new, so new that he could still smell the scent of newly sawn timber and the odour of fresh paint. Moreover, when he sat on the bed the mattress did not sag and creak like the one he was used to in his narrow quarters in Silver City. The cost of staying at the Station Hotel was, of course, being paid for by the county.

He stowed his bag and made a politic decision. The choice was open to dress as he had always done when he was on one of his missions, showing his hand in one go, or to wait and see what happened. When dressed to carry out his missions he always wore his five-pointed star in a prominent position on his lapel, boldly showing exactly who he was to put some kind of fear into those who were committing their wrongdoings.

There was something wrong, though, with this particular situation, something that told him it should be handled with a great deal more tact than a confrontation and a shoot-out in the middle of a street. Instead he elected to continue wearing the muted browns and greys in which he had been clad during his trip. This was the way in which he intended to operate for the next few days because he was not going to take action until he had to. That way there was a chance that he would not only stop the alleged corruption that was happening in this town; he would also preserve his own life and save his ranch in the bargain.

Although he had never been to Deming before he knew that it was already a thriving town to which thousands had been drawn by two things: the railroads and gold. There was a third one, too: silver, but the above reasons were the cause of the area's prosperity and problems at the same time.

Now that he was settled in his hotel and had the key to his room, which he fastened securely to his belt with a metal clip, Tucker was ready to go and have a real conversation with Frank Mars. He knew where he stood with the one and only sheriff of this prosperous town that could become a city in a few years, but he was not a man to hesitate when he had the weight of authority behind him.

He was in a brand new town and that feeling of unreality was upon him as he walked out of the railroad station and headed towards Cody Street, off Gold Street, where he would find the sheriff's office. He knew that at some point they would have to meet with the town officials, but first he needed an in-depth talk with Mars to establish precisely what was going on around here.

He was not stupid and did not immediately suspect Mars of being involved with what was going on. Like many

44

of his kind, Mars' reaction could simply have been that of a dog in the manger, a manifestation of wounded pride at the fact that someone else could have been sent to clear up his mess.

But before he headed to the sheriff's office he went to the town livery, a large building not too far from the railroad station, and went inside to purchase a horse. The livery was supposed to be the place where horses were left while their owners were in town, but he knew from experience that some of the owners never returned for various reasons and that the owner, or at least workers in the livery, would have a spare horse or two for sale at any given time. The livery, which was called Springer's, was a large and well-kept establishment. Despite the coming of the railroad, or indeed because of it, such businesses were thriving because visitors to the town still needed a way of getting from place to place, and horses were the fastest way getting around.

The attendant, a somewhat taciturn Mexican whose name he did not catch, sold him a large, solid-looking grey mare called Mags, with whom he was quite happy. He also obtained a saddle and other trappings from the livery, because such things were always obtainable even though officially they did not sell such accoutrements.

Once up on his horse and riding through town he was able to admire the area more effectively. Deming was located, he knew, in the upper Chihuahuan desert, and was thousands of feet above sea level – someone had told him five thousand feet, a fact that he found difficult to believe. The air, though, had a somehow thinner feel to it and the sun burned more fiercely as a result, while the nights could be icily cold. Unlike most deserts, water was not a problem. To the north were the Cookes range and another set of hills known as the Black Range. Often there would be heavy rainfall during the monsoon season and the waters would pour over the plains. The water would be carried along the arroyos and would sink into the ground, creating huge aquifers. These were worked by the windmills that could be seen all around the town, so water was never a problem for the people of Deming.

Tucker wondered what would happen to the railroad when the floods came, but he had already noticed that the rails and even the station had been well banked above the flat ground, which would provide a great deal of protection should such a situation occur.

The streets were wide and well laid out for visitors and locals alike. One peculiarity that he noticed – but not much of a surprise given the nature of the area – was that many of the streets were named after minerals. Thus there was Gold Street, which was the longest and ran straight through the middle of the town, and this was intersected by Silver Street. Other streets had names like Tin Street, Pearl Avenue and Diamond Avenue: just about every valuable stone or ore you could name was represented in the street names of Deming.

Many of the other streets were named after trees. There was a kind of longing in this because this area of New Mexico did not tend to have much in the way of woodlands – indeed, the lack of trees was one of the reasons why Deming had been erected so quickly on the site of an earlier mining settlement. With little to cut down in the way of forestry and no old tree stumps to clear, the community had been constructed quickly. The new avenues were called Beech, Ash, Oak, Birch and Elm and other tree names, perhaps reflecting an unconscious bias towards such things from the people who had settled there.

Paradoxically the sheriff's office was in the one place named after an individual – Cody Street. Like most of the buildings around here, the sheriff's office was a long, low detached structure made from a mixture of local red stone and adobe that he already envied, because it was not only bigger and newer than the one in Silver City, but it was also not hemmed in by various businesses. With a place like that as a retreat, a man could get things done, reflected Tucker as he hitched his horse to the post outside beside the one that obviously belonged to Mars.

When a man takes up the law he learns to look at things in a different way. Part of this is through his training and part of it through sheer experience. When a lawman is as old in the job as Tucker he instinctively knows when something is wrong – and it was all to do with the doorway. Again, like most of the buildings around here, the front of the building had wide eaves, with a square portico in front that stuck out even further. This meant that the door was in a permanent shadow, a boon to a hot and bothered man who was bringing in a prisoner, but this doorway was a deep black, meaning the entrance was wide to the world.

As a rule, a building of this kind was never open to the wider world – in fact when the sheriff was not there it was always locked, and the locks were good solid ones, the kind you would get on a trunk containing valuables. When the sheriff was in the door was kept closed, because prisoners were often kept in the gaol part of the building and their compatriots might not be too happy about this and try to free them. Altogether an open door was not a good sight.

Tucker waited patiently for another human being to emerge, but again nothing happened. The hairs on the back of his neck began to rise and a gun appeared in his hand almost automatically. Dead men tell no tales and he wanted to be in a position to shoot first.

He stepped from the bright sunshine and into the shadow of the portico, and then went through the door, but stepping in sideways so that he did not present a large target to anyone who might be in there. There was an occupant but he was not going to say or do much, because Frank Mars was lying on the ground, arms and legs sprawled out in a pool of blood, with a knife in his heart.

The first person to arrive at the scene of a crime is usually considered to be a suspect. In this case, the first arrival – after the person who had done the deed – was a representative of the law. Tucker was not, by nature, a demonstrative man, but as he looked at the body of his old friend there was a look on his face that promised short shrift for whoever had carried out the deed and a few unbidden curses rose to his lips.

Whoever had carried out the treacherous act had left swiftly and the actual office seemed intact. When he looked around, even the shotgun was still lying on the large pine desk at which Mars would have sat while doing his duties.

He did what any lawman would have done and squatted down beside the body and examined the corpse of his old friend for clues. He noted only that Frank's hands had traces of blue cotton on them where he had clutched at someone's shirt. The body was barely five feet away from the desk, and he was probably even closer to the desk when he was stabbed.

Tucker stood up and went back to the doorway. Whoever had done this had been known to Mars. Frank had come back here and was awaiting a visit from the new arrival, Tucker. When the person had come into the office he was someone who was known to the young sheriff; that was immediately obvious. Mars had stood beside his desk greeting the new arrival, who had stepped forward, pulled out the knife and had stabbed him straight in the heart.

Instinctively the sheriff had put up his hands and clutched at the new arrival as his dying heart failed to pump the blood around his body. The assailant had stepped back, and as he (or she) did so, Frank had fallen backwards and died on the spot while the assailant had walked away calmly, leaving one narrow footprint in the blood that was now congealing on the dusty floor.

Tucker went over to the desk. The shotgun lay there and he looked at it for a few seconds, then picked it up and spoke almost lovingly.

'You'll see to whoever did this.'

There was a list of local people pinned to the wall, all written in a neat hand that looked almost like printing. Mars had been a tidy man.

Tucker looked around the building, moving with speed but with a degree of caution, this time with the shotgun in one hand and the Colt in the other. His face was now expressionless but the manner in which he moved was swift and decisive; he was not a man to hang around.

He discovered immediately that the cells did not hold any prisoners. This was probably because the town was so new that most of the bad behaviour had not yet had time to manifest itself – or because Mars was not in the habit of arresting people he should have. Also, it was a weekday: most of the crimes tended to take place at the weekend when people were drunk and took out petty squabbles on each other.

When his search proved that he was the only occupant of the building, Tucker took the keys from the dead man's belt and made sure that the building was secure before he left to get the doctor whose name he had seen on the list.

Doctor Marrott was a small man in his forties with a quick and anxious manner. He was dressed as his trade befitted, in a black suit and white shirt with a crosstie around his neck. He put on a dark pilgrim's hat that went with his outfit and he carried with him a valise of brown leather in which he kept all of his medical instruments. He had been taken aback by the arrival of the newcomer, but had readily agreed to go with Tucker to the scene of the crime when the latter showed him his badge, which he always carried about with him. It was a crime to imperson-ate a state official, and few went down that route for fear of reprisal.

They went back to the jail together and the doctor looked over the body. He could not, of course, add much to the observations made by the experienced lawman, but he was able to produce a death certificate on the spot.

'Oh dear,' he said, 'a most distressing crime. A young man just setting out on his career . . . His young lady will be so upset when she hears.'

'Young lady? What's her name? How can I get hold of her?' There was a sudden realization in him that if he could not deal with Frank, he could speak to those who had known him well and get the problem of the town dealt with, not to mention finding a killer.

CHAPTER SEVEN

The Silver Dollar – saloons with the same name prolifer-
ated in the different parts of this region – was, like most of
the buildings in Deming, brand new. It was a traditional
saloon with a large, well appointed floor area and a stage
on which ladies would cavort nightly while semi-clad in
costumes that revealed more than they concealed and
alleged comedians told jokes with a local flavour. The
tables and chairs were fairly basic, as they had to be,
because that way they could be replaced quickly and
cheaply when one of the inevitable fistfights broke out on
a Saturday night. The patrons tended to be miners who
had ridden in from the hills, men who were eager to
spend the money they had gained in the form of silver or
gold ore or gold dust gained from panning. Most of them
lost their money, even if they made quite substantial sums,
because such saloons with their booze, gambling, girls and
shows were designed precisely for that purpose.

A figure dressed in the finery of a prosperous citizen
weaved his way amongst the tables and up to the bar,
where he faced another man who, at that time of day – it

was barely ten in the morning – was obviously the owner of this salubrious establishment.

'Are they here?' The barman merely nodded, opened another bottle of whiskey and escorted the new arrival through to a back room kept aside for this purpose. Such rooms sealed away from the light of day and dimly lit by oil lamps were the places where serious money could be made, because they were used for gambling, usually by card sharp professionals taking money from miners who did not know they were swimming with sharks.

The barman left and Wishart sat down with the bottle of whiskey in front of him and looked around at his companions. They were the leaders of what he inwardly called 'his' men. Even internally he refused to use the word 'gang': he was the leader of an organisation, and as such they were businessmen who were enforcing a few simple rules, that was all.

The men seated around the table were Chas Hardin, Cal Murphy, Seb Jarrett, and Jack Mason. They were all looking at him with varying degrees of disquiet. One final person slipped in and sat with them, Ruiz Montero, who wore a faint expression of surprise too.

'Well, for sure you've surprised us and us with a lot of enforcing to do,' said Cal Murphy. Murphy actually looked as his name suggested he would. He was a big blunt Irishman who had never lost his accent, even though he had been a small child when his parents came to America as part of the diaspora that had seen over a million Irish people displaced from their country of origin. He was an ex-soldier who had fought in many of the battles of the Civil War and liked nothing better to boast of his exploits when he had a few rums inside him.

'Aye, what he says is right,' said Mason, who was a much younger man than Murphy, but who also had an accent that had not originated in these shores. He was slim and fair-haired and might have seemed of Scandinavian origins, but was actually from the western isles of Scotland that had been settled by Vikings hundreds of years before his eventual birth and leaving the wild lands of Caledonia. Jarrett and Hardin said little. They were men who had ridden the trails in their youth and they were used to the long miles of comparative silence except for shouting at and rounding up their beeves, so they had developed the habit of being taciturn and only saying what was needed. They both dressed like cowboys too, with their dark shirts, wide-brimmed hats and robust corduroy trousers. They were both looking warily at the man who did not call himself their leader, but was nonetheless.

Montero said nothing either: he knew that he was there by the forbearance of the assembled Anglos. Yet strangely, he was the only one who actually came from these parts. His family had been farmers on the outskirts of the mining town that had been turned into Deming and his local knowledge and tireless pursuit of money had helped the enforcers so much that in many ways they would not have succeeded without him.

'Murphy, Hardin, all of you: you'll get what you want,' said Wishart, sitting down and looking as if he was going to an expensive show in his fancy clothes. 'The unvarnished truth is that our operation is in danger.'

'Who from?' demanded Murphy, 'I thought we had this

town sewn up tighter than an ant's ass.'

'Picturesque though your metaphor might be,' said Wishart, who had picked up some fancy learning on his journey through life, along with a fondness for Dickens and Shakespeare, 'the fact is that when an unknown element enters the situation this carries dangers for all of us. Explain what has happened, Ruiz.'

'Frank Mars went out early and met up with a stranger,' said Montero. 'They were nearly hugging when I left them. They really knew each other well; you could just tell by the way they were together.'

'They parted soon after,' said Wishart.

'I always knew Mars was a weak link,' said Murphy. 'He had some lame-headed notion that we wasn't right for the town. It's not as if he don't get rewarded well for what he was doing.'

'Well, exactly,' said Wishart. 'Small town official doesn't receive a great reward for his efforts, even wants to get married, but despite all the dangers of his job is not receiving the money he deserves, so we make a business deal with him and he gets a monthly supplement to his wages that can help him get together and marry the girl of his dreams.'

'When I came to see you, you told me to track this guy down and watch what he did,' said Montero. 'I tracked him down all right – to his office. Mars, he's dead. Stabbed to the heart.'

The reaction to this was immediate. There was a stirring around the table and Wishart banged his glass down.

'You eejit! What did you want to do that for? I told you to keep an eye on him, not to do him in.'

Montero looked at the faces of the assembled men. The truth was he would never be one of them, no matter what he did. He swallowed and spoke slowly to make his meaning clear, a glittering look in his dark brown eyes that showed he was not about to argue.

'I am not stupid,' he said, 'I found the sheriff there, but I didn't kill him.'

'Then who did?' demanded Wishart. The question hung heavy in the air.

Tucker was not a sheriff for nothing. He did not take his position here for granted. Frank Mars, he had gathered from the doctor, was a young man who had been well liked in the community. In the eyes of Tucker, that meant that anyone coming here fresh and finding him dead was immediately under suspicion of having carried out the act. Whitehill was some miles distant, and had his own city to run, so he couldn't just drop what he was doing and come over to Deming to vouch for his lieutenant. This meant that Tucker was in a parlous position. It was not unknown for feelings to run high in this part of the world and for people to be lynched out of hand. At the very least some kind of confrontation would mean that he – Tucker – would be the one who was being run out of town.

It was a situation in which he had found himself several times in the course of his career, and one in which he lived the old cliché by saying internally that it was time he grabbed the steer firmly by the horns and wrestled it, metaphorically speaking, to the ground.

The first thing he did was stride out of the sheriff's

office, which he locked, and went to get the best undertaker in town. The undertaker, J.J. Marsh, who had a
bald head and a strangely cheerful air compared to most
in his profession, was quite happy to go back with them
and help take the corpse to the morgue attached to his
building.

This was done swiftly, and as it was still early in the day
and early in the week when people were busy going about
their business and there was little or no trouble in the
streets, it meant that with a discreet carriage drawn right
up to the door of the office, they were able to transport
the body quickly and easily, with only Tucker, Doctor
Marrott and J.J. Marsh in attendance.

Tucker knew that the news of the death was bound to
get out fairly quickly.

The three of them stood in the morgue. The pathetic
body lay on a wooden slab, the knife still protruding from
his chest. The doctor felt it was wise to leave it in since, as
the murder was so recent, pulling the weapon out might
allow more blood to gush out of the open wound.

'I've issued the death certificate,' said the doctor.
'Murder by person or persons unknown.'

'Leave this to me,' said J.J. Marsh. 'I'll have his body
cleaned up and I'll suture the wound so he's all sealed up
and ready for the viewing.'

'Do me a favour,' said Tucker, 'once you get the knife
out of Frank, give it to me. It has a polished bone handle
and a slightly serrated edge. To me it looks like it was a
cherished possession, and it might jog someone's
memory.' He nodded to the undertaker and left after
being satisfied that measures were being taken for the

viewing and the quick burial of the deceased. No one hung around with funerals in these parts, as the new-fangled refrigeration hadn't really reached New Mexico yet.

'The chief suspect is you,' said Doctor Marrott, looking at Tucker with an air that showed the new arrival had not yet been exonerated.

'If I was the murderer I'd have to have balls of steel to do what I'm going to do next,' said Tucker. 'Believe you me, Marrot, I'm not about to let this rest. Frank was a good man.'

'He was,' said the doctor. 'A really good young man, with most of his life ahead of him.' But there was something about the way that the medical practitioner spoke that made Tucker narrow his eyes. One of the reasons why he was still alive after some of the adventures he had gone through was because he took note of what wasn't being said as opposed to what was.

'There's a "but" in there, Doctor.'

'I have to go now,' said Marrott, 'I'm always busy in these parts; I have my regular rounds and the mine works need a visit.'

'Spill it, Doctor.'

'I can't spill anything,' said Marrott. 'I didn't know the sheriff that well. I can only tell you that people change and they sometimes make judgements, and take an easy route that isn't so easy in the end. Now, excuse me, I have to go.'

Tucker did not argue with the doctor. There was no time for them to have a deep discussion of anything. He fetched Mags and rode away from Cody Street and the now locked building, for which he had the keys, and headed straight towards the mayor's office.

The beauty of the town being so small, and his habit of picking up on locations – a trait that had saved his life several times in the past – led Tucker to South Gold Avenue and the brand new building built out of honey-coloured stone that housed the mayor and his people.

CHAPTER EIGHT

Tucker hitched his horse beside the rest and walked towards the building. Having lived in the southwest for years now, he knew that there was a formal approach that had to be taken here, and that someone like the mayor would concede to meet him if he went through others first. So he was not surprised when he knocked on the red-painted door and it was answered by a young lady who was fresh and slim, with big dark eyes and a look about her that said she was the one to go through to get to the mayor.

'I need to see Mayor Barkis,' said Tucker, who had, of course, found out who was running the town, at least on a formal basis, before making his trip.

'Why would that be?' asked the young aide, who looked at him with a faint hint of condescension – something that Tucker hated.

'Would you just ask the mayor to let me see him?'

'Mayor Barkis is a busy man.'

'Well, perhaps he won't be so busy when you tell him

that there's been a murder in his town – the death of an elected official.'

'Who could that be?'

'Frank Mars,' said Tucker bluntly. The young woman lost her haughty air and scuttled off. Moments later Tucker was being ushered into the mayor's office. He noticed, however, that a young, tough-looking man had appeared seemingly from nowhere and also came into the office, standing behind Tucker without exchanging a word. The mayor, it seemed, was careful when it came to his own personal health, meaning that anyone who tried to put a bullet in him would wind up dead first.

The office was not particularly large and the huge, solidly built desk took up a good part of the space. It did not look so much like a desk as a solid buttress against the outside world. On the desk was a paperweight in the shape of a globe flattened at the bottom, and it was strewn with papers and had an in-tray full of letters, some of which had been opened with a silver letter-opener in the shape of a dagger. The chair on which the mayor sat had a long back and the seat was padded for comfort. Behind the mayor could be seen a bookcase in which the works of Shakespeare and the Bible were prominently displayed along with bound abstracts of town meetings, maps and other documents, while atop the bookcase were pictures of the mayor's family. The window that let the light in was not large, and there was a blind that went about halfway down to keep out the hot midday sun.

Barkis was a big man with a look of prosperity about him. This was not just an act; Tucker knew that the mayor was a big landowner who had benefited hugely from the

61

coming of the railroad to Deming. In person he had a bluff and easygoing manner, and a grandfatherly look about him accentuated by his balding pate and the wisps of grey hair around his bald skull. He did not fool Tucker for a moment. He knew they were considered a necessary evil but in general he disliked politicians, seeing them as manipulative, double-crossing men who would do any-thing to get power.

'So, who am I addressing?' asked Ted Barkis, looking at straight at Tucker with unflinching brown eyes.

'Dan Tucker. You may have heard the name.'

'I certainly have, Mr Tucker. It's my business to know about the law in these here parts. Haven't spoken to Whitehill for quite a while.'

'Harvey sends his regards. Now, I guess it's about time we got down to business. I arrived here early this morning and Frank Mars was waiting for me. He ordered me to turn tail and leave town; can you think of a reason why that might happen?'

'I don't know those kinds of details. Frank must have had his reasons. So why are you asking me this?'

'He had his reasons, Mayor Barkis. Yet Frank is dead. I went to have a talk with him at the town gaol and he was lying there, murdered.'

'Murdered?'

'Yep, murdered.'

There was a sudden hardening of Barkis' expression, and for a moment Tucker was able to glimpse the ruthless politician behind the grandfatherly image.

'You've found a dead lawman? How do I even know you are who you say? This could be some kind of act.'

Tucker had been expecting this kind of reaction. He reached into his breast pocket and pulled out an object he normally wore with some measure of pride, a five-pointed silver star. 'That's my badge of authority, and I have documents that prove I am who I say, including a handwritten testimony from Harvey Whitehill. If, as you say, you're old friends, you'll have seen his handwriting before in one form or another.'

'Your documents could be fake.'

'Sure, and if they were they would be a last resort, but I'm coming into the office of the most powerful man in town and declaring my identity. As a bluff, I would say it could backfire badly on only one person.' Barkis considered the matter for a few seconds, and it was clear from the look on his face that he had been considering the matter.

'You're here to see me to get the authority to continue with the case.'

'I am.'

'Say I sent you packing. What would happen?'

'Something like the events of San Elizaria: Harvey would send in the US Marshals with full authority to act on behalf of the territory.'

The mayor lit a cigar and puffed deeply as he thought over the matter. He made his decision within five puffs. Blowing out a thick cloud of smoke in Tucker's direction, he leaned forward at his desk.

'All right, I'll give you the authority if it's going to cause that much trouble, but I have to tell you this isn't going to go on for much longer. I'm pressing for this area to become a Luna County and entirely separate from

Harvey's little kingdom.' The look on his face did not bode well for whatever suggestions a representative of Whitehill might want to make.

'So you're going to give me the authority to act as a temporary acting sheriff for Deming?'

'This is a good cigar,' said the mayor thoughtfully. While they were sitting there – or rather Barkis was, because Tucker had not been invited to sit – Tucker noticed something strange. There was a ladder in the corner of the room, on the right when facing the mayor, and this led up to a hatch in the ceiling. This observation alone told him that perhaps not everybody was happy with Barkis being the incumbent of the office, and that the genial-looking mayor was perhaps adept at securing a way out in the face of hostile visitors.

'Well?' demanded Tucker. The mayor leaned forward and the desk groaned under his not inconsiderable weight.

'I think you'll find this is a new community,' he said. 'Everyone is pulling together. Your allegations are just what they seem to be: a series of guesses that this community's being strong-armed.' He scribbled a few words on a piece of linen-based paper, the kind that could survive the limpid heat out here. 'Take this and go. I'll give you a few days, then you're out of here.' He sat back, looked at the ceiling and continued to smoke his cigar.

'Thank you, sir,' said Tucker, in ironic tones, knowing that this was about the highest level of cooperation he could expect. He turned to go and then looked back at the man who had barely granted him enough time to begin a real investigation.

'Mayor Barkis, just one thing: Frank Mars was murdered. Now I know that could have been personal, but it's
an odd coincidence it happened jut as I arrived in this
here town. Think on that.' He said nothing more, but
flung out of the building and onto South Gold Avenue,
where his horse was still hitched up and waiting patiently
for him to appear.

What he had said was preying on his mind as he untied
the knot that held her reins to the hitching post. Mars
might well have been killed by a relative of someone who
Mars had arrested, arraigned and had hung. Such things
were not that common in the mining camps because of
the simple fact that the miners were usually loners or
worked in partnerships or small groups of three. This
usually meant that the bond between such men was not
that great, so that if one was arrested for being drunk,
stealing, or murder, the other ones usually melted away
into the background.

Deming was different, though. This was a town in which
people had put down roots. This was a community that
might have been created by the railroads, but it was still a
community where groups of people were connected by
blood ties in a way that just did not happen in the mining
camps. This meant that it was just conceivable that Frank
Mars could have raised the hackles of one of the groups to
the extent that he had been killed.

Tucker got on his horse and rode down South Gold
Avenue. It was a prosperous street consisting of buildings
built in the traditional manner, but with stucco fronts,
some painted in dark yellow or red, but most just white-
washed. This was an area where the sun shone for most of

the year, so whitewash, which was cheap, did very well in such an environment.

There was a hardware store that had tables out on the pavement containing their wares, such as metal dishes and tools for the miners, and signs that read 'Only 50 cents! Come inside for more bargains.' Another sign proclaimed 'Gold dust and ores accepted in kind.'

There was a post office – a sure sign that a town was on its way up – an assayer's office, and a claim office where people could register an interest in a piece of land.

As Tucker rode along slowly, taking in these signs and thinking about the hotel where he was going to live – because he certainly did not intend to go back and use the sheriff's quarters – there was a thought in the back of his head about what the mayor had been saying. There was something not quite right in the words Barkis had been using and it was nagging at the back of his mind, but once more Tucker was quite happy to let the thought stay where it was. He intended to continue with his investigation of his old friend and to do that – after finding somewhere to stay – he was going to visit a young lady.

CHAPTER NINE

At that moment Kathleen was sitting in the Metrople Hotel wearing a fine print dress covered in a pattern of roses that went with the real rose in her lapel. Her hair had been piled artfully on her head and she looked both voluptuous and businesslike, if such a thing was possible. She had gone to her father, the manager of this establishment, and explained to him that Wishart, who was acting like some kind of dude, had asked her to dine with him. Her father, a short, stout man in his later forties who wore a beard that rendered his expression fierce but belied his true nature, had immediately asked her to acquiesce with the wishes of his guest.

That was the only reason she was here. She did not like Wishart: there was something about the man that made her hackles rise; but she was well aware that in business, one sometimes has to get into bed with some strange partners – not that there was going to be any bedroom activity involved here, despite what Wishart might think.

Wishart turned up still dressed in the ridiculous clothes that showed he did not need to work; the contrast with his rugged features was remarkable. He doffed his tall hat as he appeared, put his gloves in the hat and hung them from a nearby stand as was *de rigueur* in such cases, and gave her a small bow of acknowledgement.

'Ah, Kathleen, *des fleur* of my heart! It's so good to see you again. I hope I have not kept you waiting for long, I'm afraid I had . . . er . . . other business to deal with.'

'That's fine,' she said, 'because I live here; I can sit down at any time.' She was trying to put an icy tone into her voice, but she was not that kind of woman, and she was able to see that he had at least taken her feelings into account, and there was something intriguing about him. He was different from many of the men who had tried to win her heart since she had developed into a full woman, but her life had been centred on her father and the struggle to establish the business in Deming since the loss of her mother five years earlier. She had to leave to sort out business for her father, but now she was back for good. She even managed to give the newcomer a convincing smile.

She knew that a man likes to be seen with a pretty woman, and that was as far as this relationship would go. They sat through a meal that was surprisingly good, considering this was supposedly a frontier town – with even salmon included on the menu. Being close to Mexico and quite far away from the sea, the inclusion of fish would not have been possible just a couple of years previously, but this small change was just one proof of the ties the railroads had made with the coast.

Wishart was unstinting in his praise of the menu, and although she wanted to eat little, she found that she ate just as heartily as her companion. Wishart spared no thought for expense – why should he, given his position? He ordered the best champagne available to go with the meal. Kathleen promised internally that she would just take a sip to keep him happy, but again found herself enjoying the taste of the drink and became aware, gradually, that she was becoming as light-headed as the bubbles that arose from the sparking beverage.

At the end of the meal he toasted her again, and was about to order another bottle of wine, but she dissuaded him from this, aware that the members of staff were already looking at her wining and dining with this guest and judging her in the process. However, she was feeling light-headed and his next words would have alarmed her if she had been entirely sober.

'Can you come upstairs with me? I was up very early this morning and I feel a little tired. Time for what our Mex friends call a little *siesta*.' In a more sober state she would have called over a male member of staff and asked him to do the deed, but her thoughts condemned that action right away. William, as she was now able to call him in her own thoughts – it had always been Wishart before – had been nothing but a gentleman since meeting her here. He had wined and dined her and he was a busy man, doing whatever his business was; no wonder he was feeling tired.

'I will need to leave the dining room before you,' she said. 'I will meet you at the stairs.' With this she rose and walked out of the room. Again, the champagne made her feel lighter than air; there was a feeling as she left that she was not quite touching the ground. Once in the main atrium of the hotel, she remained beside the grand staircase and waited until he appeared, and only once they were part of the way up would she allow him to take her arm to steady him.

They got to his room door and he stood there, his tall hat in one hand, and gave her a close-lipped smile, obviously reluctant to display his bad teeth. He swayed a little too obviously as he fumbled with the key.

Having come down to earth, she gently pulled him aside. 'Let me do that for you.' She undid the lock and the door swung open behind her as she turned towards him. 'This is goodbye, Mr Wishart, and thank you for a lovely meal. If I say so it was one of the best—'

'Just a little kiss,' he said, leaning in towards her. This was the limit for her. She had promised him a meal and nothing else.

'No,' she said at once. 'You are a guest and I did this to please my father, but nothing else—' but her words were cut short and she gave a breathless squeal as he rushed forward and propelled her right into the room across the floor and onto the bed. Turning in a manner that showed he was in full possession of his faculties, he slammed the door shut behind him, turned again and threw his not too delicate body atop the temporarily stunned girl. He was intent on one purpose and tugged at the hem of her dress to pull it upwards, while he fumbled at the front of his fancy pinstripe trousers.

Fortunately for her, two things were happening at the same time. The manufacturer of the trousers seemed to have included an inordinate number of buttons to fasten them at the front, which meant that he was having some difficulty getting his fly open, and this was distracting some of his attention from holding her down, and the

70

second was that her head had cleared and she remembered his earlier groping attack on her with a shameful clarity that showed what a fool she had been. With a cry of anger she heaved upwards, removing his weight from her just long enough to slide off the bed. Fortunately in his eagerness to get to her he had not been able to remove the key and lock the door from the other side.

She heard his voice cry 'Kate' after her faintly, but by then she was racing down the corridor and heading for the stairs. She would never go near him again.

CHAPTER TEN

Tucker halted in front of the new hotel in the centre of Deming. He was impressed by the building for a number of reasons. To start with, it was five storeys high. He knew they were experimenting with tall buildings in places like New York, but this was a tall structure for this region where buildings tended to be one or two storeys at the most. To the sheriff, the Metrople was a clear indication of intent by the railroad companies that they were going to make something of this town. Buildings like this did not appear for nothing. The main doors of the hotel were made of wood that had been stained such a deep brown that they were almost black. The inset glass on these doors was covered in designs in silver that showed a Spanish influence; hardly surprising in an area like this that had once been ruled by that very nation. As Tucker went through into the main foyer of the hotel he noticed that on either side of the door sat Greek-style urns with sculpted and painted fruit atop comprising red and green grapes, apples, and even a melon, signifying richness and abundance.

The floor was covered in a kind of chequered pattern

rather like a glorified chessboard, but with brown instead of black squares and little diamond shapes at the corners. The entire area was roomy and spacious, even when including the reception desk, which was large and solid, made of stained wood the same dark brown as the doors, with room enough for one or two clerks to man the area. Tucker was conscious of the way he looked. He had cleaned up on his arrival at the Deming station hotel, but he stuck out in these clean, bright surroundings as a plainly dressed cowboy-like figure.

The desk clerk looked at him with a question in her brown eyes. She was clearly of Mexican extraction and probably could not afford to stay in the very building within which she was employed.

'I need to speak to a Miss Kathleen Anderson,' said Tucker.

'Miss Anderson is the daughter of our proprietor,' said the girl. 'She's usually busy.'

'I need to speak to her right away,' said Tucker. There was something about his quiet authority that impressed the girl.

'I saw her dining with a guest just a short while ago,' said the girl, 'I'll see if I can get hold of her.'

Tucker sat in one of the chairs in the foyer as he waited for her to return. The seat was padded and comfortable, covered in green cloth. He was tired from his adventures and he dozed off for a second, only waking with a start when the girl stopped in front of him.

'I am afraid Miss Anderson can't see you; she's in her room and doesn't want to be disturbed.'

'Her room's at the top of the hotel isn't it? Number

510?' he said quickly.

'No, 23, downstairs,' said the girl. 'I'm afraid she won't see anyone just now.'

'That's fine,' said Tucker. 'Maybe I'll just stay and have a drink.' He got up and sauntered through to the well-appointed bar to the right, which was entirely separate from the restaurant.

The truth was, he could have done with a good beer. It was his contention that few problems in the world could stand in the way of a pint of cold beer. It relaxed a man and allowed him to be at ease with his thoughts.

He was on duty, though, and had an old-fashioned idea in his head that work and play did not mix. He waited until the desk clerk was busy elsewhere and made his way to the very room he had tricked her into telling him about. He stood outside the door of number 23 and knocked quietly but firmly. There was no response, so he knocked again, and this time he said her name.

'Miss Anderson? I need to speak to you.'

'Go away, or I'll tell my father about you,' she said, speaking at last. This seemed to him a childish response to someone wanting to speak to her, but then again he did not know what had prompted her response.

'I don't know who you think I am,' he said. 'My name is Dan Tucker and I'm here because I need to speak to you right now.'

'I don't know you,' she said from the other side of the door. 'Go away.'

'I'm the sheriff of Silver City,' he said in measured tones, although truth to tell he was becoming highly irritated by her reaction to him, 'and I've come to talk to you

74

about Frank Mars, your fiancé.'

'What about him?' There was a perceptible pause and the door was unlocked. The light from the window behind her illuminated the girl. He saw that she was in her twenties, with long, fair hair and pale skin that betrayed her Scandinavian ancestry. His first thought was that she had been crying, for there was a distinct redness about her eyes. His second was that Frank had landed well before his unfortunate demise because she was an extremely attractive woman, with not just a beautiful face, but curves in all the right places.

'Can I come in and talk?' he asked. 'Normally I wouldn't but I have news that does not bear being said in a hotel corridor.'

'I'd be an idiot to let a man I don't know into my room,' she said. 'Tell me your news right now. What is it? Where's Frank?'

Sometimes words are not needed and this was one of those situations. Kate, of anyone, knew the dangers of Frank's profession out here on the frontier. As he looked at her with those piercing blue eyes, his expression told her everything she needed to know and a low moan of despair escaped from her, her knees gave way and she fell to the ground.

Tucker might have been just above middle height and not particularly muscular looking, but he was hardwired to take action and had a sinewy toughness that had been cultivated by his life on the plains. He picked the girl up without much difficulty and laid her down on the flowery counterpane. As she lay there, being a man – and one who was good at making observations – he could not, even in

75

these circumstances, help thinking what a fine looking woman she was, soft and scented and beautiful. He wondered what she had seen in Frank and shrugged: Frank had been youthful and keen, and maybe that was enough.

The girl's eyes fluttered open and she gave a little cry of alarm when she saw a man standing over her, not seeming to recognize for the moment that he was the same person. Tucker remembered her earlier stricture about not wanting him in the room and retreated to the doorway.

'Sorry, Miss Anderson, but I couldn't leave you lying on the ground.'

'What happened?'

He owed her some information but he spared her the gory details and spoke in a calm, measured voice, coming imperceptibly closer as he did so.

'Frank was murdered in his own office. I was the one who found him. Now, before you become alarmed, I'm a sheriff too. If I were his killer I would hardly come and see you to break the news, would I? I'm sorry for your loss. He was . . . He seemed a fine young man, but I need to ask you a few questions.'

'Why?'

'Often people say things when they are with their girl that they don't say elsewhere. They see her as a confidante if that's the word I'm looking for. Did Frank say anything to you about what was going on?'

'Frank, he was . . .' her voice trailed off. 'We hadn't been on speaking terms for the last few days. Now I'll never get the chance to make up with him.' She dissolved into tears again. He fought the urge to sit down and put his arm around her and comfort her. He sensed that at the

76

present time that was the worst thing he could do.

'Frank, he was dealing with some men who've come into town,' said the girl. 'He wanted to save for our wedding, I refused to live in the sheriff's quarters after we married and my father isn't a rich man.'

Tucker said nothing but looked around what to him was a fairly opulent room, with carpeting on the floor and velveteen curtains on the window. She caught his look and hastened to explain.

'My father's only the manager of this establishment, looking after it on behalf of the railroad company. As for those names you're talking about, so many people are coming and going in Deming right now that I can't remember them all, except he mentioned someone called Jack Mason and another called Cal Murphy, then he clammed up.'

'You seem to have an issue with his associates. Do you know where they're staying?'

'Those two are living on the other side of town in opposite lodging houses. Frank, he's involved in some kind of crooked deal. I saw him, you see. I was banking and he didn't see me, but I saw him pass a whole sheaf of dollars across the counter at the First National Bank.'

'Perhaps he was saving for your marriage.'

'That's the whole point: his wages are paid by the authorities straight into his account. Frank shouldn't have any money to deposit at all.'

'Did he see you?'

'No. I had just come in the door and there was a queue, and I left immediately as if I had other business. That's when we fell out, when I questioned him about it later.'

'You've given me some names and a location,' said Tucker. 'That's good enough for me. I'm sorry for your loss, Miss Anderson.'

'Where is he?' she asked almost fiercely, wiping the tears from her fair cheeks.

'At the undertaker's,' said Tucker. 'In point of fact, I'm just going there to retrieve the murder weapon.'

'I want to see him.'

'I'm afraid I'll have to go alone,' said Tucker. 'This is territory business. Whatever Frank was involved in was bad news for the people of this town, and Frank himself. You can't get involved.' He saw the glare that she gave him and nearly smiled. She was a spirited girl, despite having collapsed at the news of her fiancé's death. 'Goodbye, Miss Anderson. I'm sorry for your loss. Frank was misguided but he didn't deserve this. The funeral will be tomorrow; I've asked the undertaker to make the necessary arrangements.' He nodded to her and closed the door, striding away with more knowledge than before.

Left behind, the girl sat where she was with a determined set to her face. Shock and grief were quickly turning to anger. She got up and changed out of her finery and into a practical shirt and riding trousers. What Tucker did not know was that she had been a rider since early childhood and liked nothing better than to trail around the area with her gelding. Whatever he was about to do, Tucker was not going to be on his own. She slipped regretfully out of the hotel because she knew that she was letting her father down, and went to the stables at the back. These were for the private use of the hotel, but most kept their mounts in the livery. She waited what she thought was the right length of time and left for the undertaker's. She was going to go and see Frank for one last time.

CHAPTER ELEVEN

Wishart did not move for quite a while. His heart was beating rapidly and he wanted to get up, go after the girl, grab her by that long silky hair and teach her a lesson about what it was like to defy a real man. Having taken in his fair share of alcohol – Wishart knew he'd had far more than the girl – and being less able to cope with it in his late thirties than in his twenties, he found that his desire to get up from the bed was negated by the way his head felt. He calmed down, and a few minutes after attacking the girl he was asleep. He had taken his siesta after all.

When he awoke half an hour later, Wishart was cursing his earlier act quietly. Not that he regretted, as he put it in his own head, trying to make love to the girl. After all, it was what most of them wanted from a man, particularly at that age, but the girl had not seen it that way and she was likely to complain to her father. Anderson had been a useful source of income, but if his daughter went to see her father and raised the matter it might well be that some unpleasantness could arise.

This thought gave him the impetus to get out of his

bed, wincing at the sudden pain that shot across his fore-head – the alcohol having made him pay – and made his way downstairs. There was a clear thought in his head: what he would do first was apply the hair of the dog to his situation, and then he would go straight to the girl's father and have a word with him and remind Anderson that they had made an agreement.

He would strongly hint that the girl, if she had made her complaint, was making a mistake, but if there was a misunderstanding between them then Anderson could rest assured that Wishart would not go near her in any shape or form again. He went down to the bar and stead-ied his nerves by carrying out the first part of the process, downing a couple of whiskies in rapid succession. Then, feeling better, he went back to the main area to speak to Anderson in his office. As he went to the foyer his eye was caught by a man who was just going out of the main entrance. The young desk clerk was still there and he went up to her as the man left, the ornate door closing behind him.

'Did that man say who he was?' he asked the girl.

'Yes, that's Dan Tucker. He wanted to speak to Kathy, but when I said she didn't want to see anybody he went for a drink instead.' The desk clerk was unaware that Tucker had actually spoken to Kathy.

'Thank you,' said Wishart, but with a look on his face that showed he was taking no pleasure in the exchange. For a moment he seemed to have an impulse to chase the man who had just left, but he quelled this and went to see Anderson instead. The thought of Dan Tucker, of all people, being here in Deming was a disquieting one.

81

*

Jack Mason was not a man who lazed around all day. Neither was his partner Cal Murphy. It was plain that the pair of them had business to get on with, and like most people in the district they rode to get to their destination. Murphy was on a robust-looking mustang that he had whimsically named Fang, because a more placid animal could not have been imagined. Mason was on a large chestnut quarter horse called Buster, who looked as if he owned the whole place, and would sometimes take a nip at any horse riding beside him just to show that he was the boss.

Both men were dressed in a manner that did not greatly distinguish them from many of the miners who passed through the district, with low, wide-rimmed, slightly battered hats, striped shirts, long cotton trousers dyed black in one case and brown in the other, and held up by braces beneath their black waistcoats. Both men were armed, with a holster on their right sides containing the traditional Colt .44. It was an expensive weapon that many of the miners could not afford, but although they did not look it, under the leadership of Wishart they had both become prosperous men.

'What do you think of the new arrival?' asked Mason.

'I reckon we ignore him about as much as we need to,' replied his companion. 'He ain't going anywhere soon and neither is Frank. I say we get this afternoon's business over with then get back for our dinners and just sit on this thing.'

The pair rode up to the meat market. This was a large,

new building in the middle of town with stuccoed walls and a sign that proudly proclaimed 'Deming Meat Market' in neatly painted black letters above the wide entrance. This was where the townspeople, the miners and others passing through would get their supplies of beef, pork and poultry, and because of this it was an important part of the town, and the railroad company had invested heavily to make sure it was going to be a solid part of it.

As the two men arrived and dismounted from their horses they were met by their associates: two younger men who had a look about them that said they were street bodies of some kind. They were young men who could have been miners but who had chosen another way of life altogether.

'So they won't pay?' asked Murphy, with a look on his face that indicated he was expecting the correct answer for being dragged out here like this.

'That's right,' said one of the young men, 'Mr Karbodis, the head butcher, says he will see you in hell first.'

'Then I guess we have to see that he gets a little lesson in etiquette,' said Murphy. 'Bring him out the back and we'll have a little chat with him.'

The gentleman in question was taken out to the back of the meat market where there were many outbuildings and stock pens. Mason went with them. He did not actually take part in what occurred there, but he gave detailed instructions for what should be done with the man, while Cal Murphy waited out front and smoked a thin cigar while looking up and down the street. His job was simple enough. When they were finished, the man was brought into the back shop where the employees of the loose association held him up. Karbodis was bloody about the nose and it was obvious that one of his teeth had been loosened, but it was also obvious that other things had been done to his body, perhaps involving hitting him with heavy objects, because he could hardly stand and had to be held bodily so that he was face to face with his new interrogator.

'I hope,' said Murphy, throwing away the end of his cigar, 'that you'll see sense now. There's more where that came from. We'll be expecting an extra payment from you due to all the trouble you've caused us.' He realized that Karbodis was looking at him with a kind of amazement; this was tinged with the purest hatred he had ever seen from one of their victims.

'You can't get away with this,' he said. Murphy stepped forward, and instead of shouting he spoke softly, almost lovingly, in the man's ear.

'But you see, we can do what we want.'

'It is not the law.'

'It's our law and that's all that counts in this prosperous little place.'

'You hurt me, but paying you is not right.'

'Well, you live not far from the premises, me lad,' said Murphy in his faint Irish accent. 'Tell you what, if this wee encounter isn't enough, we'll make your family join the celebrations. How's that for a wee idea?'

'No, do not touch them!'

'Then ye'll do as we ask.' It was a statement, not a question.

'I will,' said their victim in a hoarse whisper. Murphy turned to his companions.

84

'Ye see, lads, the gent here has seen sense. We'll give him enough time to get the money together and we'll be back later in the day. You can let him go now, lads.' The two men holding the butcher upright let go of him and the man's knees buckled under him. He fell to the ground then, by an effort of will, forced his weight onto his knees and looked up at them. He said nothing, but the hatred on his features was still there as they walked calmly out of the market, going round the back and to the front of the long building out the side, then to their horses. They were not as blatant as to walk through the market itself and attract undue attention to their deeds.

'Thanks, me lads,' said Murphy to the men who had turned up to help them out. 'Ye'll be well rewarded for your work.'

'And you'll get all the sausages you want,' said Wishart, almost jovially. The men left, grinning at this little sally. Murphy looked at his companion as they rode away from the scene.

'I hope you didn't break any bones.'

'No, I made sure they worked him over. He'll be bruised in one or two places, but nothing's broken,' said Mason. 'I always believe in keeping something in reserve, but by cracky he was a stubborn one.'

'Well, when the news gets out it'll just be good for us,' said Murphy, 'the rest of the spalpeens around here'll know to keep in line.'

'Aye, they will,' said Mason, a man of action rather than words. The two of them rode off in comfortable silence, with the knowledge of a job well done.

CHAPTER TWELVE

Ruiz Montero was surprised to see Wishart for the second time that day. The Mexican lived in one of the less salubrious parts of town, where the buildings were more or less shacks with two rooms or even less, and were built out of any materials that might come to hand. Some of them were roofed with the corrugated iron that came from the mining camps, and often the walls were made from discarded rubble from the mines mixed with brick and adobe. Montero resided in one of the better buildings with his mother and father, who had been forced to give up their farm when it was discovered that there was gold on the land. The farm had been leased from an owner who resided in Silver City, so they had not been entitled to any compensation. The money that he made from his association with Wishart was not something of which he was proud, but it was his way of supporting his family; and there was a girl he wanted to marry, and money was an issue there too.

Wishart looked disdainfully around the area where the burning of coal and the smell of crackling grease from the cooking pans in the shacks gave the air a thick smell redolent of poverty.

'What brings you out here, boss man?' said Montero with that slight edge of humour he always employed when dealing with his superior. Wishart, who had changed his clothes to a more sober dark-green suit, still looked out of place around here with his clean fingernails and polished boots of Spanish leather.

'I want you to do me a favour, Ruiz. That man you saw so early this morning, he is not someone I want around here. Neither do I particularly want to meet him at the present time. Could you do me a favour and keep an eye on him? I see you're going to speak. . . . Don't worry; I just want you to track his movements. You'll still get paid.'

'It seems a small task.'

'Small tasks can be important; will you do this for me?'

'Yes, I will do that thing, *señor*.'

'Good, now do you know where he is staying?'

'Yes, at the Station Hotel.'

'That's fine. As I say, track his movements for the next couple of days and report to me regularly.'

'*Sí señor*.'

Wishart began to walk away.

'Señor Wishart,' said Montero.

'Yes?' the dude turned and looked at his employee.

'Did you have Sheriff Mars killed?'

'No, I can assure you I didn't. He was useful to us, too useful. Montero, step carefully: we are in danger. I can sense it. This Dan Tucker, he's a lawman through and through. We can only take the necessary steps and hope we can get rid of him peacefully.'

'Or what, *señor*?'

'I have to go.' Wishart got into a coach, of all things, that headed back towards the hotel. Why would he hire a coach just to come across town? Such things were expensive to hire, and he certainly didn't own one yet. But as the young man watched the vehicle move away there was a sense inside him that Wishart had been scared – but surely not of this new intruder?

Montero was left with a task he didn't understand, but one more congenial to his nature than extracting money by force. His task was going to be easy, or so it seemed. It was a thoughtful young man who went back to the shack he called home.

Tucker soon found that he was back at the undertaker's. J.J. Marsh was a prosaic man and they met in the atrium of the funeral home because Tucker, cautious as ever, did not want word to get out before he was ready for it to happen. He knew in his heart that this situation was like a boiling pot with a lid on it. Sooner or later a head of steam would blow and the lid would fly off. This was an exercise in damage control.

'Do you want to see the body?' asked Marsh.

'No thanks, Mr Marsh; the way things are at the moment I can't tell much from a dead body. I could tell more from the circumstances surrounding his death.'

'Such as?'

'His killer had long, narrow feet. I could tell that from the boot print in his blood. Also he knew the person who killed him.'

'Why would you say that?'

'It's obvious: there was a shotgun on the nearby desk, and it was loaded. If he had been faced with a stranger he would have had it in his hand ready to defend himself. Also, he was stabbed through the heart with a folding buck-knife. That would have had to be taken out quickly and the move executed swiftly, which meant that Mars did not have time to move back, meaning in turn that his killer was close.'

'Well, here it is.' Marsh handed over the black-handled knife, which had been cleaned up, and Tucker hid it in a trouser pocket.

'Thanks. We'll make the funeral announcement today. I guess you could drop a notice off at your local paper.'

'The Deming Headlight? Sure, but that's something you can do.'

'Do me a favour: keep my name out of this. I need names for whoever might be behind this.'

'I can give you names,' said J.J. Marsh in bloodless tones, as befitted his profession. 'Do you really think this is the only violent death that's happened around these parts recently?' The undertaker looked around furtively as if someone might be lurking in the shadows, and the funeral home was indeed a shadowy place, especially when compared to the bright, harsh sunlight of the New Mexican day. 'Cal Murphy and Jack Mason,' he said in tones that were barely above a whisper.

'Where do they live?' asked Tucker.

'The bottom of town, right across from each other,' said Marsh. They're in lodgings, just like . . .'

'Just like who?'

'Sheriff, I don't want to say any more, and I guess I feel

mighty sorry that I've said as much. Now I would deem it a great honour if you would leave these premises.'

There was a sound of rattling hoofs outside the building, the sound of a horse being ridden at great speed. The sound stopped abruptly and Tucker immediately went into an offensive posture. He drew his six-guns swiftly by putting his hands across his hips, the butts of the guns facing in such a way that when he grabbed them they fitted snugly into the palms of his hands. When he drew the weapons a second later they were already loaded. Marsh blinked because, to his startled eyes, it seemed that the guns had leapt into the man's hands like flowing quicksilver.

Tucker was far from finished. He gave Marsh a swift nod to pull away from the doorway, which the undertaker did with surprising speed, for he was not a young man, while Tucker backed against the wall on the left hand side of the door so that anyone coming through would be faced with armed resistance.

A slight figure came into the building with a light but firm step, wearing a broad-brimmed hat as protection against the skin-reddening sun.

'Halt right where you are,' said Tucker, and the figure froze.

'Turn around real slow,' he said. The figure turned, but as it did so, reached up a slim arm and pulled off the hat, allowing fair hair to flow down to her shoulders.

'Do you always greet visitors this way?' asked Kathleen Anderson.

'What are you doing here?' demanded Tucker.

'You have no right to question me,' she said. 'I don't

want to talk to you. And you're pointing a gun – two guns – straight at my face.' He had to admit that she had a point and he tucked the weapons away. There was no shame or contrition in him; he had just been taking precautions.

'I want to see Frank,' said the girl coolly, turning to J.J. Marsh.

'Are you sure, Miss?' Marsh had come forward now that the perceived danger was past. He had retreated into the shadows of his own building, not wanting to join his clients next door. 'You might be very distressed about this.'

'Show me.'

Tucker, feeling as if he had become invisible in the face of this determination, followed the two into the morgue. Frank lay on the wooden slab still naked, but covered in a rough cotton sheet. He was, of course, beyond complaining about these dire conditions.

The girl turned to Tucker and raked him with her eyes. She suddenly seemed to recognize that here was the answer to whatever had caused the untimely demise of her fiancé.

'You will find whoever did this and kill them.'

'That might be the case, Miss,' said Tucker. 'Unfortunately the law says a man has a right to a fair trial, so I can't just go around blasting at people willy-nilly.'

'Then he'll never get the justice he deserves.' She looked him up and down again. 'I won't rest until I've found out who did this, and they're going to die.'

'You,' said Tucker, with a sudden energy that seemed to come out of nowhere, 'will go right back to your father's hotel and do exactly what you've always done: help out your father. Bad enough that his daughter's man has been

91

killed . . . then, added to this, she should put herself in danger? If you refuse I'll march your there myself.'

The girl could see that he meant what she said. She turned and stood over Frank's body.

'Goodbye,' she said, and kissed him lightly on the forehead.

'I'll get you back to the hotel,' said Tucker. 'Then I have my work to do.'

'Don't you trust me?' she asked, and strode out of the building. Tucker nodded to the undertaker and followed after. He liked spirited women, but had a feeling that this young lady was heading for more trouble than she knew.

Time would tell.

CHAPTER THIRTEEN

The funeral of Frank Mars was held the next day. The death of a sheriff was a big thing in a town like this and caused a stir, with the story featuring on the main pages of the Deming Headlight. Tucker, by dint of visiting the editor, had managed to keep his name out of the newspaper. He wanted to keep his anonymity in order to function better at his job and, knowing that he had the backing of Mayor Barkis, the editor had agreed. There was a great deal of speculation about who the murderer might be. Mars had two unofficial deputies, both given stipends by the town, but both men had been at their daily occupations when the murder occurred and both were shocked to the core by what had happened. Neither of them, as it turned out, was willing to step into the breach and both were willing for Tucker, who had interviewed them by the time the article appeared, to step in and carry out the work for the moment.

The funeral was held later that day in the Deming Congregational Church. The church was a fairly large building, reflecting the fact that the railroad company was willing to accommodate the simple Anglo faiths. Not far from here there was also a synagogue and a Catholic church, because religion was important out here in the southwest and most people went to church on a Sunday, unless they were working in the local silver mine where the shifts were constant.

The interior of the building was simple with little in the way of decoration. The seating, which consisted of folding wooden chairs, could be cleared away so the building could be used for other purposes, such as meetings of the young mothers' society. The pulpit was raised up from the rest of the hall, with a red varnished wooden cross at the front. Behind and beside the minister there was an area where the choir could stand, and to his right was a lever-powered church organ at which sat the obligatory elderly church member: a lady who knew how to play the thing.

The minister, who oddly enough was called Dr Service – his degree being ecclesiastical, rather than medical – was a tall, thin man who, although he was married, looked as if he might disapprove of most of the pleasures of the flesh.

The hall was crowded but Tucker did not attend the funeral openly. There was a small side room where the minister could hold private meetings with his congregation, which looked on to the body of the hall, and it was here by dint of an open door and through a decorated screen, with help of J.J. Marsh, that he was able to identify those whom he would regard as the main suspects in the case. Marsh had shown a willingness to help and had passed the actual labour of the funeral on to his assistants.

The coffin was carried in by a number of friends of the

sheriff, who seemed to have been a popular man because the church was bursting at the seams, and the minister carried out a long funeral speech. The men that Marsh pointed out did not sit together but dispersed themselves around the building, mixing in with the rest. It was notable that at least two of them were given black looks by other members of the congregation.

Kathleen sat at the front beside a stout, small but peppery man in a good suit, this being her father. She burst into tears when the pine coffin was brought in and her father had to comfort her. The speech seemed interminable, but the side room did not have any other way out so Tucker just had to sit there until the ceremony was finished. J.J. Marsh emerged unobtrusively and assisted his men to take the coffin to the black-painted carriage. Even the horses were wearing black plumes, made out of ostrich feathers. The procession departed for Mount View cemetery, which was on the higher slopes above the city, and was a pleasant area that indeed looked towards the mountains.

Tucker was a man who worked by association. Now he was able to match the names he had been given to faces. As he went back to what was now his office, unobserved and without remark since he barely stood out on the bustling streets of the new town, he considered his options.

Once the funeral was over – it was ending with a gathering at the Metrople where guests would be served coffee and cake – the congregation would disperse and they would all go about their business.

He decided that he could wait another day for what was

to be an arduous task.

He was going to confront the men who thought they secretly ruled this town.

CHAPTER FOURTEEN

Tucker was always an early riser, believing in the old adage about that which enabled the early bird to obtain breakfast. His mind was set on what he was going to do, but he was going to show this part of the world more of the real Dan Tucker than he had revealed up until now. It was six in the morning when he arose. He had a wash in his room and a shave with the hot water brought to him by an equally early-rising member of staff. As he dressed he looked in the mirror. What he saw there was a man of slender build with light blue eyes and fair hair, turning to darker brown. He remembered when he was a child he had often played so much in the sun with his brothers that his hair had been bleached almost white.

It had been easy for him to keep out of the public eye because of his naturally retiring disposition – almost shy, some might have said. This natural lack of ostentation was what had helped him to survive so well in his job, but now it was time to make a public declaration. He donned a blue flannel shirt made of good material, a solid protection against the cold morning air. He also donned long, light-coloured calfskin boots into which he tucked the legs of his dark overalls. Atop his shirt he wore his customary black waistcoat cut away from the side so he could reach the guns on his hips, the handles turned in the opposite manner from that which might be expected so he could cross his arms and draw them out with a speed that had to be seen to be believed. He wore a large, dark sombrero with a patterned band. This would hang down his back, supported by a thick leather string as he revealed his face to whomever he was speaking. The hat was a weapon in itself, for when worn during the middle of the day it shaded his eyes from the harsh New Mexican sun and kept his head from overheating. Then he donned the silver badge that he had worked so hard to earn.

The last item he picked up was one for which he had obtained a number of shells the previous day; the object of his attention was Frank's shotgun. He looked at this for a moment, picked it up and strode out of the hotel and into the still cold air.

Finally, he donned a pair of soft tan-coloured gloves, also made from calfskin and lined with sheepskin. He was under no illusion of how cold it was outside.

His horse was still in the livery. Cursing Tucker roundly under his breath, the balding Mexican got Mags ready, and as Tucker rode out into the streets of Deming he could see from the town clock that it was still well before 7 a.m. He was not alone as many of the citizens were up to open their businesses while others were heading for the mines.

98

The rooming houses about which he had been informed were on the other side of town. This area looked respectable enough, with one of the two local schools being located nearby. Both of these buildings were in red brick, as were the boarding houses. The railroad companies must have invested a lot of money in attracting people here, perhaps even giving them land and building grants, because all of these buildings were substantial.

Tucker went up to the door of the rooming house on the left hand side of the street and stepped back. A middle-aged, pleasant enough-looking woman answered, protesting at the early hour, and Tucker had a brief word with her. Then she disappeared inside and a moment later an unshaven man appeared in his shirtsleeves and hastily donned trousers, his feet bare inside his unlaced shoes.

'Jack Mason?' asked Tucker. In one hand he held the black-handled knife, but the man looked at it with an indifference that was clearly not faked.

'Yes it is!' snapped the man, evidently annoyed that he had been disturbed in the middle of a good sleep. The swollen bags under his eyes and the redness of his face attested to the fact that he had been drinking and doing other activities until early in the morning.

'Get out of town,' said Tucker. He put the knife away and lifted the shotgun and pointed it at the head of the man. 'This is a fair warning; there won't be a second. And take your men with you.' He shifted his lapel so that the silver badge glinted in the early morning light. He turned without another word and heard the door slam behind him, but there was an audible 'click' as it opened again as he made his way over the road. He strode straight across the way and carried out exactly the same process at the opposite boarding house.

This time the man who appeared seemed to be made of harder stuff than Mason.

'Yes, I'm Cal Murphy. What's it to you?' he asked. Tucker also gave Cal a clear view of the knife but he, too, did not seem to recognize it, so Tucker put it away and hefted the shotgun again.

'Get out of town and don't come back,' said Tucker, also pointing the gun at his head. 'You've got twenty-four hours, all of you.' He said this loudly enough to reach the man who had come back out unobserved and now stood in the opposite doorway. Murphy froze as if he was a statue of himself, but there was a terrible certainty about his attitude that showed the sheriff's suggestion was not going down well.

'Aye, and you'll be the man,' said Murphy before also slamming his door. Tucker was already on his steed and riding away when he heard a door opening again and someone running across the road. He did not bother and kept going, for he knew exactly what was happening. The gang members were going to speak to each other.

Tucker had waited to investigate who his foes were. Now he was doing what had to be done. In his own mind he was giving them a fair warning about what would happen to them if they did not obey his injunction to leave town as promptly as possible. He also knew that arriving so early to deliver his warning would mean that he would have caught them when they were at their most disorganised. This was why they had not rallied to fight him back immediately, and it was also the reason why he had ridden away so promptly on Mags. Besides, he was a busy man and had to get to South Silver Street as quickly as he could.

The buildings at this end of the street looked less salubrious than those on the north side of town. There was a slight air of neglect about them and one or two shanties could be seen amongst their smarter neighbours. However there was one substantial ranch-type building near the end of the road. He dismounted from Mags and hitched her reins loosely to a rail and rattled his fist hard against the door, producing a noise like a good-sized thunderstorm.

Whatever you might want to say about the criminal profession, they did not seem to be a type who got up with the lark and the miner. Such were their powers that they seemed more concerned with the midday prowl and night-time gambling, and so it was with his latest catches. A bleary-eyed landlord, who wore an interesting grey nightgown, was sent off in search of Messrs Hardin and Jarrett.

He heard the landlord comment, 'There's a man to see you; he seems pretty steamed up about something,' and this was enough to get them to come to the door. They were perhaps in fear that their leader had appeared, so it was with some astonishment that they were greeted by a man who bore the office of sheriff. As for being 'pretty steamed up,' the landlord had judged Tucker purely by the depth and verve of his knocks: Tucker was completely calm, with only the shotgun in his right hand to indicate that this was not a slightly early social call.

'Hardin and Jarrett,' he said, his icy blue eyes drilling into them. 'Just been paying a little visit to a couple of guys you might know. Got the same message for you as I

101

had for them. Get out of town as soon as you can. You're not permanent residents, so with all your baggage you should be able to depart in twenty-four hours. Make sure you do so.'

'Who says we'll do what you say?' Jarrett demanded rather than asked. His hair was on end and he looked as if he had seen a ghost, but this was due more to being ripped at an unearthly hour from his comfortable bed rather than because he was frightened of the new arrival.

'One more thing.' Tucker reached into the inside of his waistcoat and produced the black-handled knife. He gave a flick of his wrist and the blade gleamed in the early morning light.

'Either of you scum buckets ever seen this before?'

Jarrett was looking at the knife as if transfixed. He was not a great physical presence, being somewhat on the weedy side, and he had dark bags under his eyes.

'Get lost,' said Hardin. 'We ain't leaving, are we Jarrett?' But Jarrett said nothing and Tucker turned to walk away from them. When he was a few yards away he heard Jarrett break his silence for the first time.

'We'd better tell Wishart what's happening right away.'

'Shut it up, idiot,' was Jarrett's response. Tucker kept walking, sheathed his shotgun in the leather holster fitted to the saddle, got on his horse and trotted down Silver Street back to his temporary home. He had a lot to mull over, and one of the things he had to think about was that name. It was not one that he knew, but a man like that did not appear from nowhere. There was a certainty in his mind that this Wishart was not who he pretended to be, so

102

why shouldn't one of them be someone he had known before?

He would soon know the answer.

CHAPTER FIFTEEN

Montero was at the Metrople not long after Tucker had carried out his warnings to those who had been told they had to leave town. In order to track Tucker, Montero had taken up residence at the Station Hotel. His room, of course, was his for free. The management of that establishment were also paying Wishart and his cronies a goodly sum of money to be left alone. The way the management looked at it, if they caused ructions and tried to oppose the criminals, the new station was such a key factor in attracting visitors that the kind of publicity surrounding a huge confrontation would be hugely deleterious to their business. This worked on the same principle as a saloon getting known as also being a secret whorehouse, meaning that more respectable clients would shun the business if they got to know this was happening on the premises.

Montero walked out of the Station Hotel. It was just after seven in the morning.

Shortly afterwards he arrived at the Metrople and went inside. Soon he was in the large room that had been commandeered by Wishart and facing the very man who lived and slept there. Wishart was far from the dandy he had been a couple of days before. He was dressed in a plain black morning suit with a wing collar and string tie. He looked a great deal more businesslike than before. He was also disgruntled because he had not yet had his morning bath and the girl had been avoiding him like the plague.

'This had better be worth it, sonny.'

'Mr Wishart, Sheriff Tucker ... he got up and went to see these people, your leaders,' said Montero. 'I followed him but went down the back street and waited at the back of the buildings. I heard him tell them to leave town. Then he goes to the commercial district and the boarding house on Silver Street. I saw him confront Hardin and Jarrett from a distance. I did not need to hear what he said.'

'He didn't see you at all?' Wishart seemed to grow paler by the moment.

'No. The first time I was sneaking behind, and the second I saw from a distance. He seemed too busy to notice me.'

'So you weren't followed as far as you know?'

'No.' Wishart looked like a man who has just breathed the deepest sigh of relief in his life.

'All right, that gives us some time.'

'To do what?'

'To meet and make our plans. Sheriff Dan Tucker is going to die.'

Tucker was in his room at the hotel and calmly preparing to go to the office that had become his. He had hired a woman to clear up the mess at the scene of the crime and now he was going to take over on a full-time basis. In addition he was going to have to go back to his deputies and ask them to drop their day jobs and act with him full time. The two men, Kremsky and Bailey, both worked in the main area of town. Kremsky was a carpenter and Bailey was a barkeep, both vital jobs in the economy of a town like this one.

There was a knock on the door.

A couple of hours had passed since his morning trip but it was still early and there was no need for a staff member to disturb him at this time. This must mean that the person was not a member of staff. Tucker got up from the bed on which he had been sitting. He had taken off his gun-belt while he was in his room, but the rifle was lying beside him on the bed. Was that what it was to be? A quick hit and then the new sheriff was dead? It might be a crude but effective way to rid the town of what some would perceive as an interloper.

They didn't even need to open the door and wouldn't be able to because there was a chain-lock affair on the inside to give visitors some privacy. He knew from experience that they could just shoot him through the wooden panels if they wanted, if he was stupid enough to approach the door chest outwards. He had even killed a couple of criminals in this manner before, during his other investigations.

Instead of trying to go towards the door face onwards, he went side-on and kept his distance away from the actual panels as he stood beside the green-painted door.

'Who is it?' he asked. If there was no answer then the odds were it was someone out to make an attempt on his

106

life. People did not seem to be exceptionally chatty under those circumstances. His suspicions were confirmed again when the person just knocked. With a flick of the wrist he undid the key chain and flung the door open, poking his shotgun in the face of whoever was there.

'Drop your weapon, friend,' said Tucker in his lazy drawl. There was a startled gasp which came from a distinctly feminine source, so Tucker stood in the doorway and looked full on at the girl who stood there. She was unarmed and looking somewhat alarmed.

'Kathy!' he said, looking at her with an air of admonishment. 'What in the name of the Pecos are you doing here?'

'I don't like answering questions with a shotgun pointed at me,' said the girl. Tucker had the grace to admit that this might be a barrier to socialisation.

'Sorry,' he said, lowering the weapon, 'I thought you might be someone else.'

'Well, I'm not.' The girl was looking extremely pretty in a dark blue dress that reached below the knee, as was the convention, while she wore shiny, lace-up boots with flat heels that looked practical for everyday wear. Once more he could not help thinking what a fair representative she was of the species, with her fringe of blonde hair and her wide, generous mouth and that tilted up slightly, freckled nose and those big blue-green eyes. Tucker was not a man who had much to do with the opposite sex since he did not normally strike them as being particularly desirable until they got to know his sterling qualities. Besides, his lifestyle was such that dalliances with the opposite sex were hard to come by unless those particular ladies plied their trade in saloons and, being a man with a fastidious nature, he tended to steer away from that variety of the female species.

'What,' he asked, 'do you want with me?'

'I couldn't help noticing you weren't at the church yesterday,' said Kathy. 'I thought you would have wanted to pay your respects to an old friend.'

'That's where you've got it wrong,' said Tucker. 'I was there, all right, just not where I could be seen. Now state your business, Miss, I have a lot of work to do.'

'Maybe you have.' She closed the door and approached him so that he could smell the light perfume that she wore. 'Are you going to help me, Sheriff?'

'Depends on what you want, Miss.'

'I want to help you, and that would help me. I want us both, working together to find Frank's killer.'

'You should keep out of this,' he said. 'Let the professionals ply their trade.'

'So I'm just supposed to sit back and let them get away with it?'

'You're not supposed to be involved at all.' But then as he stood there with her, a sudden thought occurred to him. 'Does the name Wishart mean anything to you?'

The girl looked at him as if he was trying to make a fool of her. 'As a matter of fact, that's a very familiar name indeed, Sheriff Tucker.'

'Why would that be?' He was made curious by the tone in which she spoke. He knew immediately that the name meant a great deal more to her than she was letting on.

'I don't want to go into details.'

'But you know where to find him?'

This time her smile was positively beatific. 'You could say that, Sheriff.'

'Tell you what, Miss Anderson, you trade me some facts and figures and I'll get you to help out with my little investigation.'

'You want to know where Wishart is? He's been living at the Metrople for months now. He doesn't seem to pay any bills, and he seems to have a hold on my father I can't explain. He's a black-hearted, evil son of a gun.' She stopped, knowing that she had been about to head into a rant about the demerits of her chosen individual. 'And you can call me Kathy, Sheriff. All my friends do.'

'You can call me what you want,' said Tucker, 'but everyone just calls me by my second name. Well, Kathy, leaving aside your personal feelings for a minute, Mr Wishart has now become part of a wider investigation. If you excuse me, I'll just have to be leaving.'

'What am I to do?'

'I'm glad you asked.' He took out the black-handled knife. 'I want you to go around town and ask a few questions about this here weapon for me. Just ask all innocent like, say you want to return it to its rightful owner.'

She reached out for the weapon and then shrank away from it. 'Is that the knife that killed Frank? Stabbed him right to the heart?'

He did not have to reply: the answer was on his face. For a moment the look of hate and scorn she directed at the weapon was enough to make him start putting it away. 'Never mind, I'll fit it into my day.' He discovered, though, that she was holding out a slender hand. He could see that she was not happy, but there was a trace of grit in her that he liked.

'I'll take it, Sheriff – I mean, Tucker. I'll do what has to be done.' She held the clasp knife as if it was as deadly as a snake, which in a sense it was, then dropped it into a hidden pocket in her dress.

'I'll leave now,' she said. 'It wouldn't do for the ladies of this town to see me coming out of a hotel with a man. The gossip would reach new heights.' He watched her go, giving her a few minutes to leave, and then he departed too, going to get his horse from the front of the building and heading towards the Metrople.

He was going to have a word with one of its guests.

CHAPTER SIXTEEN

Marshal Whitehill looked at the telegram that he had received from Deming. He read it again as if it were a joke. He was seated in the chair usually inhabited by Tucker when that person was performing his duties in Silver City. The only difference was that this time the cells had a few more inhabitants, a few lively mining feuds having occurred since the departure of Tucker to his new area of jurisdiction. Whitehill was addressing the big man who stood there in front of him.

'Well, Gladius, this sure looks like some kind of mess. I got a telegram from Tucker not long after he arrived at Deming informing me that the sheriff there, a boy called Frank Mars, has been found murdered. That worried me, 'cos it seems that these guys who have taken over Deming are getting mighty serious right away. Only thing is I know Tucker: he thrives on this kind of situation, keeps his head and gets on with it. Now I get this.'

'Let me see,' Gladius Moore scowled as he pored over the contents of the telegram. Like many of his ilk he was not greatly literate. 'Mayor Barkis has told you that he doesn't want any more interference and that this is his jurisdiction?'

'Heck, he even says *he's* going to appoint the new sheriff,' said Whitehill. He put the piece of paper on the desk and brooded for a moment.

'Can he do that?' asked Moore.

'Sure he can,' answered Whitehill. 'He has a high civic appointment; he can do more or less what he wants, 'specially now that they're making ructions over there to be called a different county. Within a year or two they want to become Luna County an' they'll be completely outside my jurisdiction.'

'Even when it comes to murder?'

'See, I think this Barkis is protecting his own patch,' said Whitehill. 'I think he knows who the crooks are and he's getting some kind of kickback from the whole thing, and in return he's giving them his patronage.'

'Strong words, Marshal,' said Moore, 'but it still doesn't explain why I'm here.'

'That's simple enough, Gladius; you're taking the next train out of here and you're going to Deming while I hold the fort here with my deputies.'

'What do you want me to do?'

'Simple: I want you to contact Tucker and help him clear out this – for want of a better term – nest of vipers. You up for that?' Moore did not look greatly enthused, but the county was paying him so he couldn't really refuse a posting.

'All right, Marshal, I'll go, but I reserve the right to act if I'm threatened in any way; and Tucker ain't my boss in this, we're co-workers.'

'Whatever makes you comfortable,' said Whitehill. Moore donned his hat and slouched out into the New Mexican sun and was gone.

Whitehill stared at the cells, not really seeing them or their inhabitants at all.

He wondered about what he had done and why he thought Tucker might require some help, and then he went over to the stove and put on some more coffee.

Tucker stood in the small space from with the supposed proprietor ran the Metrople. Not for the first time he wondered why it was that such a small man with a gingery beard had managed to produce such a beautiful daughter as Kathy. Reed Anderson looked at the new arrival.

'I want you to do me a favour, Mr Anderson,' said Tucker. 'I want you to call out your guest, Mr Wishart, so that he meets me in front of the hotel. I have a few questions to ask of him.'

'Mr Wishart's not here at the moment,' said Anderson, 'and I don't know when he's going to return.'

'Well, when he does, tell him he's got about twenty hours left before he has to leave town. If he doesn't go then he'll have me to answer to, and he doesn't want to do that.'

'Can I ask what this is about? Mr Wishart has contributed hugely to this town,' said Anderson. 'It's outrageous that you're asking him to leave.' The manager of the hotel was expressing indignation, but Tucker could see by looking at the man that a great deal of this was mere bluster.

'I get what's happening here,' Tucker said. 'There's a

113

hell of a torment going on in this town. None of the officials – Mayor Barkis, for instance, or the owners – want the behaviour of these men to be exposed for one reason only: you want to attract a great deal of commerce and a huge amount of people, and turn this into a city as fast as possible. Because of that you don't want open warfare with this Wishart and the townspeople. A lot of innocent people might get killed or hurt in the process.'

'I really don't know what you're talking about.' Anderson had cocked his head to one side so that he resembled a rather gingery parrot.

'I think you do, Mr Anderson, and you're not coming straight out with it for the very same reasons I've just given.'

'I have to go, Sheriff. We're busy, and I don't know where my daughter is. That girl's a good staff manager but she seems to have taken the day off without telling me. After what's happened I don't have the heart to go on at her.'

Tucker decided it might be wise not to mention to the hotelkeeper that his daughter was currently going around the town with the knife that had killed her fiancé to try and find out who the murderer might be. They stood at the ornate inner door of the hotel. Tucker looked seriously at Anderson.

'When you make a deal with the devil it's only a matter of time before he consigns you to the flames.'

'I am well aware of that.' Anderson looked around in a conspiratorial fashion. 'He's usually back for his dinner at about five p.m. and he dines pretty well.'

'That, Mr Anderson, is all I need to know.' Tucker gave

the owner a nod, donned his sombrero and walked out into the blazing heat of the day. Facing the hotel were the new streets of the town, replete with hardware stores, saloons and all the other necessities for life. There was also a dark alleyway to one side that led down the back of the main street, and from this there was a sudden loud bang as a gun went off and a bullet headed straight for the sheriff.

CHAPTER SEVENTEEN

The Silver Dollar was busy at noon with many customers in to get a cold beer and get away from the heat of the day. Wishart entered, still wearing his dark suit in contrast to all the finery with which he had once decorated his body. Wishart had the look of a sober businessman, which was not really that far from the truth. He had not been to the funeral the previous day and there was a pale, withdrawn look about him that did not speak well of his state of mind. Once more he went to the back of the saloon where his men were waiting. They were all there once more except for Montero who had duties elsewhere. It was evident from the look on their faces that they were not in a happy frame of mind. Having a shotgun pointed at their faces, along with the order to leave town, had concentrated their minds wonderfully.

'At last,' said Cal Murphy, who looked as if there was a sour taste in his mouth. 'What in the devil's name is happening here?'

'I think you know the answer in many ways, Cal,' said Wishart. 'We've been given an ultimatum. He's on to us big and he wants us to leave.'

'This place has been full of rich pickin's for us,' said Jarrett, 'an' now we've got to up sticks and leave because some asshole from Silver City waves a shotgun in our faces.'

It was at this point that all three of his companions began to talk at once, all giving the same story of what had happened and how this had interrupted their respective beauty sleeps, which in their cases were badly needed.

'Two things to tell you,' said Wishart. 'I've been to see Mayor Barkis. He was mighty mad at me for doing so, I can tell you. He doesn't even want a hint that he's associated with us. But I went at it from a political angle. This place is still tied in with Grant County. If he can swing it at the next election they'll get their own county. So he's messaged Whitehill not to interfere any more.'

'That's great news,' said Jarrett, 'but that ain't going to help us right now.'

'Yes it will,' said Wishart. 'I'm seeing to the problem right now. You don't have to worry about a thing if I'm right about this.'

'You're not clear,' said Murphy, looking as if he wanted to explode with anger and just keeping himself in check. Wishart gave him a tight little smile.

'Just wait for a little while and you'll find out the reason for us being here. Let's just put it like this: we'll talk about business and by the time we're finished two deputies will be in charge – and they'll do anything we ask.' His smile appeared and grew broader at the thought.

*

Tucker felt the hot sting of the bullet as it sailed past him, just barely touching his side. He had not been shot at by a professional; that was clear by the way the bullet had missed him. The other reason was because the range of the shot was from such a great distance. It was obvious that the would-be killer was trying to keep well hidden from his victim. With this in mind, Tucker did something that no one taking aim at a victim would have considered: he ran towards the source of the shot. At the same time he crossed his hands across his body and pulled out the six-guns so that they seemed to appear magically in his hands within a split second.

As he ran, a second shot rang out, and if he had kept to one speed and one direction it would have hit him square in the middle of the chest. But as he moved forward he changed his pace all the time, and he weaved from side to side, something that might have indicated to someone else that he was quite drunk. It was a method he had used before and it had saved his life more than once because very few handguns – and it was a handgun that had been fired – were that accurate unless the person was quite close.

He ran up the long alleyway that led behind the shops and was able to see that a young man was there. The young man had turned, gun still in hand, and was running away as hard as he could. Normally, for trying to take his life, the reward would have been a shot to the head. Not that Tucker was a coward who would shoot someone who had his back to the sheriff, but the young man still had a weapon and could be considered dangerous. Instead the sheriff took careful aim and shot the young man in his left leg. There was a shout of pain and the young man fell to the ground, the gun skittering away from his open hand across the alleyway.

Tucker came forward rapidly and kicked the young man over onto his back and the youth turned over with a cry of pain.

'Say, it's only a flesh wound,' said the sheriff, no trace of pity on his smooth features. 'I ought to blast your blamed head clean off your shoulders, but that's not going to happen, is it, kid?'

'Help . . . I'll bleed to death,' said the young Mexican.

'Don't worry, I'll get help,' said Tucker. 'There's a hardware store around there does bandages. We'll get your wound sorted, but you'll have to help me. Who sent you?'

'I can't tell you,' sobbed the young man, 'they'll kill me.'

'Suit yourself,' said Tucker. 'I can just let you suffer here. Who knows, the bleeding might stop.'

'I'm not a killer,' wailed the young man. 'Please, please help me.'

'Names,' said Tucker.

'I'll give them,' said the shooter, and he did.

Kathy arrived at the jail later in the afternoon. There was a look of determination on her young features and she rode towards the building as if she was on a mission. Tethering her mare to the hitching post she knocked on the door. A panel was slid aside and a pair of sharp eyes regarded her through a wire mesh. The panel was slid shut again and Tucker allowed the young woman into the building. For the first time she noticed that Tucker was dressed in a far more flamboyant manner than previously, with a sombrero that still hung down his back, that deep blue shirt, the black waistcoat and his fancy braces. It was a look that suited him and made her think of him more as a person than before, and he was a reasonably good-looking young man.

The second thing she noted was that one of the cells was occupied by another good-looking man, who was much younger. One of his legs had been heavily bandaged and he was sitting on the plank bed in the cell looking extremely sorry for himself. He turned his face away from her as she came in.

'Ruiz, what in the name of Moses are you doing here?'

'You know this man?'

'Yes. He's what I would call a runner for Wishart, a kind of glorified message boy. He would do anything he was asked to do.'

'Well, he sure did that, I guess. He's been chirping like a miner's canary and I have all the evidence I need to string up a few of his friends – including the one just mentioned.'

'What are you going to do with Ruiz?'

'It depends; he's committed a hanging offence, trying to murder a sheriff.'

'I was only trying to scare you off,' said Ruiz sullenly. 'I'm sorry. You are a good man.'

'Now tell me your news,' said Tucker, 'and perhaps if you can vouch for him, I'll show some leniency to this young criminal, meaning I won't string him up in the middle of the town as a warning.' The young man in the cell gave a sob of contrition at this information. Had he known it, he was far better where he was.

'I am well known in the town. I went around some of the trades, the livery and the meat market. I was chatty, pretended that I had found the knife and I wanted to return it to its rightful owner – in a way, that's true. It was at the meat market that I struck gold, so to speak. There was a Mr Korobodis there. I think he must be of Greek origin – his English isn't great – but when I showed him the knife he reacted quite badly. He told me it was a bad thing, a very bad thing indeed.'

'Hardly a surprise given some of the things that they have been doing in the area,' said Tucker.

'He told me that he had seen this very knife just a few days ago. He was resting in the shadow of the porch in front of the market – it was a very hot day – when he saw Frank arguing with Seb Jarrett outside on the street. The argument was getting quite heated, and Jarrett produced a knife – this very one. It has a distinctive curve to the blade and a black, textured handle. It opens up on a spring catch, and he saw Jarrett displaying it to the sheriff.'

'So now we have a suspect arguing with a man who was eventually found murdered with the very same weapon. Will Korobodis come forward and testify, do you think?'

'I don't think so; he's like a lot of people around here. He's scared of them and what they will do. He might if he's protected . . . I have the impression his life has been made a misery by them. The meat market is hugely profitable.'

'I'll give him the ultimate protection,' said Tucker grimly. He held out his hand and the girl gave him the knife. He turned toward the prisoner, who did indeed look sorry for himself. 'Montero, do you want to save your neck?'

'They'll kill me,' said the prisoner. 'They are bad; I did this all for my family. My mother, she is ill, my father is dead. . . .'

'Can you tell me if this knife belonged to Jarrett or not? Keep in mind that your answer might determine whether or not you end your miserable existence as a warning to others, strung up in the town square.' In actual fact Tucker knew that, as a captured prisoner, Montero was entitled to a fair trial, but the lawman felt that anything that helped his cause was fair game.

'No, I swear.' The young man looked up at Tucker with dark, haunted eyes. 'It is the knife that is belonging to Jarrett. He played with it all the time, tried to put fear into others.'

'That's enough for me. If you testify when all this is over, you'll have saved your own neck and I'll make sure you get a reduced sentence.' The prisoner said nothing but hung his head again. He was weakened by the loss of blood from his wound.

Tucker turned to Kathy. 'I want to thank you for what you've done today, Kathy. You've got no idea how you've helped me out with your legwork. And a fine pair of limbs you have on you, I might add.' There was a little twinkle in his eyes as he said this that showed he could still appreciate a pretty woman.

'I think you're really saying a thank you, but that's your

task finished,' said the girl.

'Far from it,' said Tucker. 'You're in a great position to help me. I want you to go back to the hotel and make sure that your father knows about Montero becoming my prisoner. Your father will tell Wishart. I've already put a warning through your father that Wishart has to leave town within the next day or so. I've given all the major players their ultimatum so it's up to them how the dice fall.'

'Why don't I just tell Wishart direct?'

Tucker looked her full in the face and once more she was struck by the intensity of those ice-blue eyes. The girl gave an involuntary shiver as if she had been bathed in equally cold water. 'I don't think you understand what's going on here. If Wishart thinks you have any connection with me at all he'll use that to try and destroy me. He's not just bad and in it for the money; he's evil. He'll hurt you, Kathy. Please keep out of this.'

'He's right,' said Montero suddenly from the corner, where his cell was. 'He was going to hurt my family unless I try to kill Señor Tucker. He's worse than bad, that one; he has been touched by the devil.'

'Just do me one favour,' said the girl.

'What's that?' asked Tucker.

'See to it that Frank's killer gets what he deserves.' She stepped forwards, put her arms around him and gave him a sudden kiss on the lips. Tucker moved back, not because he was displeased but because he did not want her remaining any longer to her own endangerment.

Tucker took the step of seeing that the outside world was clear before beckoning the girl out to the street. Kathy got on her mare and rode off, with Tucker watching her go, and for once she did as she was asked and went straight back to the hotel that was her home.

CHAPTER EIGHTEEN

Gladius Moore took the train to Deming. It was the next morning after his conversation with Marshal Whitehill, and he was not a man who hesitated in the execution of his orders. Whitehill was not a stupid man in that he had not told either Barkis or Tucker about the new arrival. He knew that, in both cases, the arrival of the additional sheriff would be rejected angrily.

Moore got off at the train station and looked around with a satisfied smile: he was looking at a neat little town, much of it brand new. He could see the money that had been invested in this town by the railroad companies, an investment of which he approved since he was a shareholder in railroad stock. If things went well in Deming they could be looking at a place that attracted untold thousands of people every year from either side of the border. Ranching and mining could only grow in this area, along with the expansion of the town into a city. No wonder they were talking about Deming becoming the new Chicago.

He stopped contemplating the future and looked instead to the present. Tucker had already informed Whitehill that he would be taking a room at the Station Hotel. Moore asked which room was Tucker's and the desk clerk – who was no callow youth, being a man in his forties – gave Moore a suspicious glance.

'Who says Mr Tucker is even staying here?'

'Tell him the sheriff's here – the *real* sheriff. Moore's the name.' Moore had been wearing a greatcoat to keep out the chill of the early morning weather. He would have to discard this as the day wore on. He pulled his lapel aside to reveal the silver star beneath. The man paled.

'Sorry, sir,' he apologised. 'Sheriff Moore, you say?'

'Yep, that's right.'

The clerk scuttled away, had a word in a back room to some member of staff and came back promptly. 'He's not been back for an entire day; seems he's holed up in his office.'

'Office, is it? What street is it on?' The clerk told him and Moore cursed inwardly. He was feeling tired from his trip and he had been looking for a little discussion with Tucker in his quarters. Now he was being forced to walk across town. It was still early in the morning because he had taken the postal train from Silver City, and it was still cold enough to wear gloves. Some bright stars twinkled in the New Mexican sky and beneath his hat his ears were cold. He walked briskly to try and get some heat. He just hoped that Tucker had some coffee on the boil.

*

Some people seem to keep to their old habits, even when those habits are ones that might make them redundant within a short space of time. Cal Murphy and his friend who was more of a co-worker, Jack Mason, had spent what was supposed to be their last night in Deming in the Silver Dollar saloon.

They had both vowed that they would have just a drink or two, carouse with one or other of the prostitutes – because the respectable women of the town knew what they were and would have nothing to do with them – then they would go home mostly sober. As it was, things didn't turn out that way.

At nine at night, which was early really, they were both at the bar having their second drink when Wishart came into the building. He was wearing the same suit that he'd had on that morning and would have looked like a respectable businessman if it had not been for his pock-marked face. It was obvious that he wanted to see them. There was a feeling of cold fury about the man that cut through the usually cheery atmosphere of the saloon, where miners were doing their best to get rid of their hard-earned gold and silver for cheap whiskey, and some girls were dancing on the stage in scanty costumes.

They played Follow my Leader and went with him to the poker room where he stood and glared at them.

'He didn't do it. Montero was supposed to kill the sheriff, then those two idiots were supposed to become sheriff and deputy, and Barkis would tell Whitehill things were settled here and that we didn't need the US Marshals to come in.'

'Well, that settles it now,' said Murphy. 'I'll just find the

127

eejit and give him a dose of lead from which no man can recover.'

'I'll back him up,' said Mason with a fine air of bravado, 'except we can get some of our men to do it, Cal. They'll do a better job than that young fool.'

'No!' Wishart gave a roar that made them jump even though they were seasoned blackmailers and extortionists. 'Don't you see? If we kill him like that, despite what Barkis says, Whitehill will say all anarchy has broken out in Deming and he'll requisition the marshals to come in after all.'

'Well, what's your fancy, Davey boy?' asked Murphy.

'He's given us an ultimatum,' said Wishart with a grin that was almost like the rictus smile of a dead man. 'Well, let him stick to his plans. You see if he's seen going about the streets trying to kill people, then the boot is well on the other foot. He's holed up now. If we attack the jail, hundreds of citizens will see us, but if he keeps to his stupid deadline it'll be early on and we'll get him right. You two get home early and wait, armed, and when he attacks make sure you put him in his grave.' He left then, a pallid sheen on his forehead and with hands that trembled.

This was not the commander they had once known: Wishart was afraid, deadly afraid and he walked with the step of a man who was marking time until his doom. So the two kept their promise in their own fashion: they left the saloon at one in the morning instead of three, as was their habit. They had taken several fewer drinks, although still plenty if anyone was counting, and they were bold with promises of what they would do to the interfering Tucker.

*

In another bar called the Golden Spur, Jarrett and Hardin waited with each other. They had already spoken with Wishart before they went out drinking, but neither of them was happy with the command. Jarrett was a lean man, narrow even down to the soles of his feet, but with a hard face that betrayed his attitude to life. He voiced his disquiet to Hardin.

'I say we just go and get him. He won't stay holed up in the place all night, will he? Let's go to the station, lie in wait and deal with him when the time comes.'

'Ambush him? We have plenty of men who do our work for us. Why don't we rope them in?'

Jarrett shook his head. 'The guys we pay off to do our work, most of 'em baulk at outright killing, and you can see why. Getting money from businesses is fine, but when they have to kill lawmen they'll run a mile. Better to keep this between us.'

'You never did like Frank Mars, did you?'

An oath rose to Jarrett's lips. 'Interfering little piece of bullcrap. I had him to rights. He was letting us do what we needed to do for long enough, and then he decided that we was going too far. He was trying to pull us back. Us! Like we was some kind of tame little posse who gave him his kickback and would turn all school ma'marmish when it came to what needed to be done.'

'I hear there was questions being asked about the owner of a certain knife.'

'Was there? Don't know nothing about that.'

But Hardin could see from the sudden stillness of the

man that he was on to something. 'Did you do it, Seb? Did you? Because if you did, just because you hated that little pipsqueak sheriff, you was breaking ranks. You know you was.'

'I'll order another bottle of rotgut,' said Jarrett. 'Barkeep, your best whiskey, and make that two bottles; we've got work to do here.' When the bottles came he slouched off to a round table where normally two men who wanted to play poker would sit.

'You an' me, we got a job to do,' he told Hardin as he uncorked the first bottle, the cork coming out with an audible pop. 'We get him and end all this. Barkis is in our pocket; he'll smooth everything over.'

Hardin had a sense of disquiet about him, and this disquiet grew even as time went on because Jarrett consumed about twice as much whiskey as his companion. Jarrett would not respond to any further questions about his involvement in the death of Sheriff Mars, and by the time they got out of the saloon it was obvious that Jarrett was in no fit state to ambush anyone. Hardin managed to get him on his horse – just – and they rode back to their lodgings at the far end of South Silver Street.

'Sure there was something we meant to do,' said Jarrett, mumbling like an old man over his chops.

'Surely is,' said Hardin. 'Bed for us both. We've got an early appointment, one we can't miss.' He was regretting staying up so late when they would have to be alert the next day, but most of all he was beginning to view Jarrett with complete loathing. A man who went around knocking off members of the law could not be considered a worthwhile companion – too much of a loose cannon.

When he reported this to Wishart, he was sure that his leader would agree. One day, and soon, Jarrett's bleached bones were going to be found out there in the hills picked clean by vultures.

CHAPTER NINETEEN

The girl got out of her bed at five in the morning. Because she lived and worked in a hotel, this was not an unearthly hour to her. Indeed, they had members of staff who were on night shift for the precise reason that a hotel never closes. There always has to be someone on duty even if the front doors are locked and bookings are no longer being taken. She had not slept that well the previous night, and she knew why: this was a morning when she was going to put her lithe body in the way of danger. This was not a pleasant thought, but it was one that was overridden by a feeling that she had to be out there in the twilight of morning with the man who had helped her identify a killer.

She put on clothes that were distinctly mannish in form – a pair of slacks, a large jumper that she used when she was out riding early in the morning, long boots of brown leather that fitted almost up to the knee, and a woollen hat that clung tight to her head to keep out the cold morning air. She felt as if she was doing a deed that was correct, despite the knot of fear inside her stomach and the fact that it was still dark as she slipped out of one of the service doors. In her right pocket was a hard object that reminded her of why she was here, and as she led her horse out of the hotel stable she could feel a tide of determination surging through her. She was going to make a difference.

A man came out of the sheriff's office as Moore appeared. The man was dressed in familiar garb and he came swiftly towards the new arrival.

'Get inside,' said Tucker. 'We'll have to talk.' He went swiftly back into the building, and when Moore followed at a more sedate angle Tucker closed and locked the door behind him. There was a look about Tucker that Moore had never seen before: being in different towns they had mostly socialised and had never made an arrest together. What he saw in Tucker was a kind of quiet intensity, a hard focus on what he was doing.

Moore noticed that Tucker did not even ask why he, Moore, had arrived. He just assumed what was true, that Whitehill had sent him to aid his fellow lawman. There was a young man with a wounded leg in one of the cells who was holding the bars.

'They'll kill you,' said Montero. 'They'll kill you both. Get out of town now.'

'Who's this scum sucking piece of dog crap?' enquired Moore.

'Not important. I see you've only got one Colt .45. Here's another. Stick it in your belt if you don't have a spare holster. Montero, shut up, or it'll be worse for you.'

'I only try to help you; they are bad, bad men.'

'Exactly,' said Tucker, implying in that one word that he was going to sort out all the bad men in town for good. He turned to his new companion.

'This ain't the biggest town on Earth. I'm riding down the road for a whiles, hitching my mare, and we're doing most of this on foot. You'll be coming in from the side to back me up, but stay as hidden as you can from the start because I know how this is going to happen.'

'I don't know what to say.' Moore was tired from his early journey and a little bemused.

'Just do what you did in the salt wars, and get things done, Gladius,' said Tucker. 'There's only one thing: don't kill anyone unless they try to kill you first, and keep as hidden as you can.'

With that, they went out of the building together. Tucker looked around cautiously as they left, knowing that many an operation of this kind had been aborted from the very start by a well-placed sniper's bullet.

Moore got a horse from the livery and they rode towards the other side of town where Mason lived in his lodgings across from Murphy. They hitched their steeds at the top of the street. Moore did as he was asked and hid in the shadows, flitting down the backs of the buildings, while Tucker walked boldly down the street. He had walked barely fifty yards when six men, all bearing arms of one kind or another, emerged and lined out across the road. It was a broad street to make plenty of room for carriages and wagons to pass, but even so, by standing there with a measured distance between them, the men were able to effectively block his path. Most of them were carrying clubs of one type or another, although one or two

134

had knives and at least one was armed. Tucker looked from one grim, silent face to another, and his own expression did not change.

'Get out of town,' said one of the men, who was taller than the rest, and seemed to be some kind of leader amongst them, 'or it will be the worst for you, Sheriff. You see, we don't want to hurt you, but we will if needed.'

Tucker kept calm in the face of what already seemed like impossible odds. He recognized these men for what they were, the ground troops of Wishart, and knew at once that the leader had been playing his cards close to his chest and had not informed those who had received the previous ultimatum of what he was going to do. However, Tucker had a policy of dealing with those at the top and he did not see any point in fighting when he didn't have to.

'Listen here,' he said with measured calm. 'I'm a sheriff appointed by this here Grant County. Now I'll give you boys the chance to go quietly, or there will a lot of trouble you don't need. I know why you took on this job; most of you came here to work in the mines for the companies or on your own, but you found that digging for gold or silver is the devil's own work. Wishart came to you in low bars, saloons and whorehouses. He whispered in your ear and he promised you a good wage for very little effort.'

The leader type, who had a wolfish grin and the only gun, looked as if he was about to snarl like the animal he so resembled.

'Now every one of you has got to know this. If you kill me, Whitehill will send in the US Marshals, and there will be no running or hiding from them. The ones they don't

135

gun down will be the ones that they hang, because you're all accessories after the fact.'

'Get out or I'll plug you in the head,' said the wolfish man, but there was now a little bit of uncertainty in his tone.

'I'll pretend I didn't hear you threatening an appointed official,' said Tucker, 'but that's the only pass you'll get.'

'He's alone,' cried the wolfish man, but there was sweat on his brow despite the cold morning air. 'Let's just get him. Who's going to know?' But the men were uneasy at the prospect of attacking someone who was a highly dangerous representative of the law. Most of them knew the legend of Tucker's boss, Whitehill, the man who had once arrested Billy the Kid in Silver City; and Tucker, with his obviously loaded shotgun and twin pistols, was a very different prospect from the shopkeepers and traders with whom they had dealt in the past.

'I ain't alone either,' said Tucker, and like an actor who was coming in on cue – although he had been hiding in the shadows all the time – Gladius Moore appeared with a pistol in each hand, while Tucker cradled his shotgun almost lovingly in his arms in such a way that they knew he would use it on the slightest provocation.

Even the wolfish leader stepped back at this new impasse.

'You,' said Tucker speaking directly to him, 'drop your gun and get the hell out of here. There's a train soon. I suggest you all get on it and clear off to a place where you don't persecute innocent people, or go back to mining. Either way, this little pit of poison is gettin' cleared.'

Wolfish grin man included, the men dropped their

weapons and Moore covered them as they ran away. Both sheriffs waited for five minutes in the cold air, but no one returned or shot at them from the shadows.

'Grunt men,' said Tucker. 'Enough brains to threaten somebody but not enough to run an operation. Thanks, Gladius. You've kind of done your job for now. Let me get these ones.'

'I'm coming with you.'

'There's only two of them down here. What if any of their men return, or there are others misguided enough to take their place? Gather up some of those weapons and get ready to fight a rearguard action.'

Moore shrugged and waited as asked. Besides, he had a sneaky feeling that even if Tucker had been on his own, he would have bested the seven men somehow. Moore had just made the process a little easier.

Tucker set off alone.

CHAPTER TWENTY

When Mason arrived home at just after one on the morning he was slightly less the worse for wear than Murphy. They were going to hole up together in Murphy's lodgings, but Murphy had determined in his own mind that they should keep watch separately, and that way if one was attacked the other should come to his aid. Now Mason was in his quarters looking out uneasily between a gap in the curtains. He was tired – extremely tired, of that there was no doubt – and there was a regular thumping in the back of his head that had necessitated the drinking of copious amounts of water, a substance that he and his friend Murphy despised. Never the most humorous of men, there was also an air of gloom about him today that he could not dispel. Along with this feeling there was a kind of anger that had been building up because he had only been able to get a few hours sleep. He wasn't going to run away though, and he had a Winchester '73 by his side, that trusted aide of so many adventurers. He badly wanted to go across the road and speak to Murphy; standing side by side the two of them could take out some pipsqueak sheriff. But in his mind he was also defiant and angry. He would take out the intruder, Mayor Barkis would condemn the actions of Tucker, Whitehill would be shamed into leaving Deming alone, and the gang would operate as before.

Tucker appeared, holding his shotgun in a light, almost caressing manner. Fired by the sight, Mason tried to pull up the shutter window only to find that the wood had swollen through dampness and would not budge.

'Come out with your hands up, Mason,' roared Tucker. 'Time's up. You've got a choice: you can get on the train outta here or you can face me.'

Mason gave a roar of rage, wrapped his hat around his fist and smashed the window to poke his rifle out, ready to shoot the new arrival. Tucker, perfectly aware of what was happening as soon as he heard the tinkle of glass, raised his shotgun and fired at the now broken window. Mason saw the weapon being raised and rolled across the narrow front room as the roar of the shotgun blast entered the room, sending glass and shot everywhere.

Tucker was standing to the right of the building. Mason opened the front door, pulling it to one side, raised his Winchester and stepped out, firing as he did so. He was very nearly lucky, because the bullet passed so close to Tucker that for a moment the sheriff spun around in a grotesque manner, staggering to get upright, but he had only been dodging the bullet.

Mason did not get a second chance. Tucker raised the shotgun, walking forward as he did so, and shot Mason in the middle of the body. Mason was still standing on the steps of the lodging house. A hole with a spreading blossom of red appeared in his chest and the force of the shot flung him backwards, his now useless rifle clattering to the ground beside him, the smell of gunpowder in the air.

'Bastard, ye bastard,' cried a voice behind Tucker. A man came out of the red brick building opposite with a pair of Smith & Wessons in his hands. But Tucker was already turning; he had heard the door being open and the clatter of the man's boots against the steps. 'Ye murderin' swine,' yelled Cal Murphy, but he was reeling a little from the effects of having just woken, and he was not fully able to concentrate his aim. Instead he let off a few wild shots, one or two of which passed perilously close to the sheriff.

Tucker, however, was not about to stand still and let the other man shoot him down. Because he was closer to the man he had just killed, the sheriff did the obvious thing and rushed into the open door, passing the inert body of Mason as he did so. The sun was beginning to come up by then and the contrast between the shadows and the sunlight meant in effect that Tucker had vanished.

Murphy was not a man who was used to employing his guns. As Tucker had already mentioned, he was more used to terrorising people by using his men to enforce his edicts. Because of this, Murphy made the biggest mistake: as he came running forward he fired directly into the open door, while of course Tucker had dodged to one side.

'Stop this!' roared Tucker, 'put your weapons down and I'll only arrest you.'

Murphy had emptied both his guns and they made

feeble clicking noises as he came forward. There was no doubting his foolhardy courage because he, too, rushed past his dead friend and ran into the lodging house.

'I'll kill ye,' he roared, 'ye heathen bastard!' Surprisingly he was able to partially make good on his promise. He had rushed forward so fast that he came upon Tucker before the latter was able to raise his shotgun again, because Tucker had been plastered flat against the wall to avoid the bullets Murphy had been firing. With an oath the Irishman closed in on Tucker with heavy, meaty hands. He punched Tucker on the shoulder with such force that Tucker dropped his shotgun. Tucker rallied and swung a surprisingly forceful, bony fist and cracked Murphy on the side of his considerable jaw. The Irishman retaliated with a vicious crack on the side of the head to Tucker that left the sheriff reeling. Tucker fell to one side and the Irishman closed in on him with a flurry of blows to the body.

The shotgun was lying in the dim hallway now, and Tucker knew that if Murphy was able to get hold of this then he would use it to end the life of the sheriff and to blazing hell with the consequences. Tucker fell back at the blows. It was no use; when close in his opponent was bigger and stronger, and he would defeat the sheriff using mere strength. This was not a happy prospect for Tucker, so he did the most unexpected thing he could think of: he fell to the ground.

Tucker's fall was not accidental, but planned. For a man of Cal Murphy's size and strength it was by no means easy to punch an opponent who was lying on the ground, and it was also hard to see him in what little light was filtering through from the open door. Murphy, however, did not see the shortcomings in what was happening and prepared to dive atop his enemy and pin him down. Lying there on his back, Tucker forced his right hand, the one that had dropped the shotgun, into play and went for his Colt .44. The weapon did not exactly leap into his hand as it normally did and for a moment he thought it was going to stick because of the position in which he was lying.

Just as Cal began to descend, the sheriff managed to get the weapon into his hand and fired. The bullet caught the man through one of his eyes, and at that range it exited through the back of his head with such force that most of his villainous brains came out as well.

Murphy fell forward, twitched spasmodically, groaned briefly and hoarsely then died.

He had not fallen straight forwards but had landed across Tucker's legs, trapping the sheriff where he was. The landlord appeared, still in his nightclothes, aware that the shooting had stopped. There was a great deal of pandemonium in the building as various guests were reacting with horror to what had happened. One woman was shouting hysterically on the floor above them. Tucker looked sharply at the landlord.

'Help get this bastard offa me,' he said.

CHAPTER TWENTY-ONE

As she came forward with her horse, the girl suddenly found that being out here on the streets was a great deal different than thinking about what she was going to do with her fiancé's killer. It was no coincidence that the gang had been able to extort so much money from the businesses of the new town. They were ruthless, determined men, and she was only a young woman with vague thoughts of revenge on her mind. She tethered her horse at a commercial building and walked down towards the bottom of South Silver Street.

Two things were on her mind – well, a great deal more than two, if the truth had to be told – but the two main ones concerned Tucker and the weapon that she had in her pocket.

Tucker had given the members of Wishart's gang a firm ultimatum. They, of course, had decided that they were not going to pay any attention to this. She was puzzled as to why they hadn't killed the sheriff like they had Frank, but she supposed they had their reasons and she would learn these in due course. There was no sign of Tucker – yet – and the daylight was beginning to loom, and she was a young woman out here on her own.

Silver Street was named for a reason: it was the longest street in town and the furthest end led to the roads that ultimately took the traveller into the Mimbres wasteland and out into the hills where, at this very moment, men were starting to dig in their relentless search for the precious metals. This end of the street had descended into shacks, shanties and lean-tos. It was not the safest place for a young woman to be in.

Had Tucker known? She took out the weapon that had killed her fiancé. When she embraced Tucker she had taken the knife out of his loose side-pocket, thoughts of revenge uppermost in her mind. Now she knew that the sheriff wasn't here, the thought was a faltering one. She paused in the shadow of one of the lean-tos. The owner was clearly not there, probably having set off for the mines half an hour before her arrival, and looked across at the place where she knew the men were staying: a more substantial ranch-type building across from this very spot.

Kathy decided that, for the moment, the best thing she could do was to wait and see. That was when the dark-clad figure of a man appeared behind her.

Tucker came down the road, and as he walked steadily towards where he had hitched his horse he was met by Moore coming in the opposite direction.

'Heck, I heard some shooting so I came running, and

144

then it stopped. Are you all right?' he asked.

'Yep. I managed to deal with them both. I'll have a bit of explaining to do, because I killed rather than made them leave town like Whitehill asked,' said Tucker. He had largely managed to avoid the gore his bullet had spilled in the boarding house but his boots were stained with blood. 'Come on, Gladius, there's a job to do.'

They both got on their steeds and headed across to the other side of town. As geography would have it, South Silver Street was about as far away as it could possibly have been from where Tucker had just had his confrontation. The trim sheriff did not express much emotion as they went away from the scene. Moore, although he was a big man, was trembling with fear at the thought of what might happen next, but Tucker was as calm as someone going for a Sunday picnic. As far as he was concerned, he was doing his job.

When they got to Silver Street, Tucker did the same as before. He tethered his horse outside a saloon and began to walk down the road, cradling his newly loaded shotgun. He kept the shells loose in his capacious left-hand pocket, and he could break open the shotgun and reload it almost as fast as he drew his pistols. When he got to the end of the road he could see what appeared to be two men fighting with each other, one being much more slightly built than the other. Then the hat flew off the slimmer 'man' and long hair streamed out and covered her neck. He realized that he was looking at Kathy.

Without saying a word, Tucker ran forward and butted the man on the back of the head with the wooden stock of the weapon he was holding. The man gave a roar of pain

145

and collapsed to the ground. He lay there and Tucker looked briefly at his upturned face. It was the wolfish-looking man from earlier, who was obviously more highly paid or perhaps more conscientious than the rest.

'Hell of a thing,' said Tucker. He looked at the frightened girl. 'Kathy, no time to talk. Get yourself hidden behind one of those shacks and don't come out until this is all over.' He wasted no further words and led the girl to a spot where she might be safe that his experienced eye picked out from amongst the low buildings. He would have led her to safety all together but he knew that he didn't have time.

He came back out to the main road and nodded to Moore, who knew precisely what to do and hid with a gun in either hand besides the building adjacent to the ranch-type hidey-hole. Tucker ran towards the ranch and halted quite a few yards from the building but far enough away to let his voice carry. 'You can come out and be arrested or you can have a shootout. Either way, we know what you've done and you're leaving town.'

There was no reply, except for the sound of breaking glass. Not being stupid enough to wait in the open, Tucker zigzagged towards the building and even before a shot was fired he was in the shelter of the spacious doorway.

These were men who were desperate. If they stayed where they were they were going to be confronted by a man with a shotgun. Moreover, this was a man who knew how to use it, and neither of them wanted that to happen. There was a noise from within the building as both men ran for the back door.

Moore, who had been watching from his shelter, saw

146

that the back door had opened and the two men were hurrying out. He took a shot at them, but because he was quite a distance away he missed by a wide mark. One of the men gave a shout of fury and raised his own gun and shot at Moore, who had ducked behind the wall. The shot kicked up splinters from the building, but also did something that had far more serious repercussions for the sheriff. He was sheltering behind a jerrybuilt construction that was not that stable. The vibration from the bullet loosened the badly constructed roof and a beam of rough wood swung loose and descended on Moore's head, followed by a stream of loosened tiles. Moore gave a groan and fell down to dusty ground, half unconscious, his body twitching as he lay there.

The two men saw what had happened and ran towards the spot so that they were heading away from where Tucker was sheltering. The remaining sheriff was now a man in pursuit. Jarrett, who had fired the shot that had caused the partial collapse of the building, paused beside the twitching Moore and began to aim at the sheriff's head, but Hardin jerked his arm away.

'No time, come on.' The way that they could have gone would have taken them out to the plains beyond, because the line of buildings was thin, just one layer deep that lined the road on either side. They had no recourse but to head into the town.

Neither of them were old – both were in their early thirties – but a combined lifestyle of booze and easy living since they had arrived meant that neither was particularly fit. Together they headed past the buildings.

Now Tucker was in pursuit of them and he shouted at

them again. 'Give it up boys; you know where this is leading.' There was some degree of rancour in his voice, but not a huge amount considering that he had seen Moore felled to the ground.

'No use,' said Hardin, 'we've got to turn on him and shoot it out.' His companion merely grunted his assent.

Neither trusted in their marksmanship enough to confront Tucker out in the open, so they fled down the side of a shack that overlooked where the man was coming from. This gave them the advantage of putting them in shadow. Hardin was the less cautious of the two. He approached the edge of the building, exposed his body for a moment and took a wild shot at the rapidly approaching sheriff.

Tucker dodged the bullet again and responded with a blast from his shotgun that would have taken off the top of Hardin's head if the gang member had not pulled back.

'Get round the other side of the building,' he said harshly to Jarrett. 'Get him from the other side.' Jarrett was wide-eyed with fear, but he was a killer too: he had killed a number of men in his time, including making one foolish move that had led to this very situation. He was not a coward, but there was something relentless about Tucker.

Tucker went around the far side of the shack in which they were hiding. It was a simple enough manoeuvre: they were trying to outflank the enemy. Even as he moved out, Tucker spoke in ringing tones. 'I'll give you a minute to surrender, guys, and if you don't it will be the end for you. Now, I don't think Moore is dead, and if he recovers you just might get prison. If you don't surrender now, you're dead.' The words were spoken so calmly and with such reassurance that they sent a chill through the hearts of the two men who were listening.

Jarrett moved around the building, immediately rejecting all thoughts of surrender. He looked out. From his angle he was standing sideways on to Tucker. But the sheriff had been listening; he pulled back and pointed his shotgun at where the man was sheltering.

'Not coming out then? You asked for it.' Sensing that whoever was to his right was the most immediate danger Tucker began to march towards the side of the building where Jarrett was hiding. This was the moment Hardin chose to rise from his hiding place and fire at the sheriff. The shot came close, and blew a hole in the sheriff's hat, bursting the crown, but it also meant that Tucker had to turn away to take care of this new menace. In his hasty attempt at killing the sheriff, Hardin had left himself fully exposed. He was lucky: Tucker was still some distance away and the blast of the shotgun took Hardin on the lower body. His legs were peppered with shot and he fell to the ground groaning and in no fit state to continue.

However, the minor shootout had left Tucker vulnerable. He had turned his back just long enough for Jarrett to come out of his hiding place. Jarrett was sweating in the steadily rising sun but he knew that he had the sheriff now. He ran forward so that he was close enough to get an accurate shot just as Tucker turned around. Both barrels of the shotgun had been used. Tucker began to drop the shotgun; once this was done he could reach for his six-guns, but they both knew it was too late.

Surprisingly the look on Tucker's face was not one of fear. Things were happening too fast for that emotion to take over. Instead he had the look of a man who was going to fight to the very end.

Jarrett lifted his pistol to finish the job Hardin had started and blow the sheriff's head off his shoulders. Suddenly he gave a grunt like a man who had jarred his back stepping off a too-high boardwalk. His arm jerked wildly and, even though he tightened his finger on the trigger, the shot that would have taken off Tucker's head just a moment ago was far enough off to make the bullet sing past the sheriff's head. Tucker was moving by then, throwing his body to one side, a manoeuvre that might have worked even if Jarrett had fired more accurately.

Jarrett spun around, gun still in hand. Tucker could see that there was a knife sticking out of Jarrett's back just above the shoulder blades – a knife with a black handle. Just beyond Jarrett, having lately come out of the shadow of the shack where she had been sheltering, stood Kathy. Jarrett's mouth was a questioning 'O' as he sank to the ground, and the gun fell without reward from his opening hands. He dropped to his knees, fingers of both hands splayed out as if he was going to use them to dig in the dusty ground, then he fell forward on to his face.

Tucker, not surprisingly, came forward and felt Jarrett's neck for a pulse. He looked up at Kathy.

'Thanks, ma'am, bit of poetic justice there. Now can you ride out and get me Doc Marrott, if your horse is still around here. Get him to bring me a buckboard so I can ship 'em out to his clinic.'

'Why?'

'Because these ones are still alive and I want 'em

patched up. Besides, this one's going to have to go on trial for murdering Frank.'

The girl ran to do as she was asked.

CHAPTER TWENTY-TWO

Wishart headed rapidly towards the railroad station. He knew that there was an early morning train that he had been unable to catch because he was waiting for his men to deal with the problem of Sheriff Tucker. Just minutes before he had heard the bad news when one of the men scared off by Tucker had come to the Metrople. The sheriff had been as good as his word, and there were other rumours of shootings down South Silver Street. He was wise enough to know when it was time for him to ship out. This particular goldmine had yielded enough money to keep him in comfort for a long time. He was dressed in a dark green suit with a faint herringbone pattern that had been made from the finest cloth. He wore a bowler hat and carried a carpetbag in one hand and a valise in the other. There was a coach and four waiting for him outside the hotel, the driver getting paid double for turning up so promptly. Money talks, even if it has been gained by force.

He was at Deming railroad station within minutes. He

was not alone either. It seemed that many of the men – and women, though not as many as the men – who had worked for him were anxious to leave the town, and were waiting under the station awning in the early heat of the day. He was wise enough not to join them, but waited further along at the edge of the station, having ascertained from a porter that the Santa Fe express would be arriving shortly.

He stood there, outwardly calm, but there was a Colt .44 stuck in his belt and a grim expression on his face, which did not alter as the sound of the train was heard in the distance, and the plume of steam could be seen like a smoke signal.

It was at that moment that Tucker appeared, coming rapidly around the edge of the platform. He was no longer clutching the shotgun but there was a determined swagger about him that caused a stir amongst the prospective passengers.

'Relax,' he said tautly, 'I ain't after you low-lives. I'm lookin' for one particular gent whose acquaintance I ain't had yet.' He did not add that he had been given a description at the other hotel of what Wishart was wearing and carrying. No one else had a carpetbag.

Wishart stood in the shadow, frozen there as if this would prevent him from being seen, but Tucker spotted his enemy immediately. He marched rapidly towards the spot and Wishart turned to face him. Tucker was relaxed, as he had to be, but his arms were resting on his gun-belt, hands in the middle, ready for action. He could outdraw any man present and they all knew it.

'William Wishart?' asked Tucker. 'I'm taking you in. Get

your goods and march.' Wishart had been enough in shadow for the sheriff not to properly see his face. Now he lifted his pockmarked features and stared back at Tucker more calmly than his situation warranted.

'Suppose I don't want to go?'

For the first time since setting out that day, Tucker showed a sign of astonishment. 'Reinhardt? Kurt Reinhardt? How the hell did you end up here?'

'Same reason you did, I guess. Something to do with fate and opportunity.'

'Last time I saw you, you weren't long for this world.'

'I survived, Tucker, no thanks to you. I survived and I prospered, but not in Telluride, and not in the mines. Not in the empty rot-pocket where you abandoned me.'

'It wasn't like that.' Tucker's face hardened. 'So you couldn't even do the honest thing and work hard.'

'I came here and I worked hard, all right. This suit, the money, all came from my hands.'

'Not honestly; not the way it should have, Kurt.'

'And what did you become, Tucker? A soldier of fortune, a murderer on your own accord? You kill for pay. I get paid to prevent violence. Which one of us is better?' Now if you'll excuse me, I have a train to catch.' He had to raise his voice as he spoke these words because at that moment the train drew into Deming station with a series of roars, clanks and hisses that all but drowned out all speech. The men and women who were leaving town began to scrabble onto the train even as the guard was beginning to blow his whistle to indicate that the magnificent machine had stopped for a short while. The story about the US Marshals coming to town had got around

154

and none of them wanted to be there when that happened.

'Guess you know where this has to end,' said Tucker loudly, his own voice not being the loudest, so that he almost had to shout. 'Drop the gun out of your belt. I'm taking you in.'

That was when he felt a blow on his back that knocked him to the side. One of the low-life men had decided to help his old boss after all. Tucker was quick to react and thudded his gun against the side of the man's head. The interfering man fell with a grunt of pain, but then it distracted Tucker from his enemy.

They were close, so close that the chance had to be taken. The man who had been known as Wishart swung his carpetbag in a wide arc. He was a powerful man and the moves were just enough, close enough to distract Tucker, especially as the edge of the bag caught him on the side of the head. He staggered and nearly fell. He fought to remain upright, swaying as he did so and shaking his head, and by the time his vision had cleared Wishart had retreated around the edge of the railroad station building and had vanished from sight. Cursing his own foolishness, so eager had he been to get his last kingpin in this sorry affair, Tucker had lost sight of the fact that a man as resourceful as Wishart was not going to give up easily.

He pulled out his guns and edged around the building, but Wishart was not going to hang around to try and kill his old enemy. He had unhitched a gelding from the front of the hotel and had jumped on its back. The owner of the horse had come running out of the hotel shouting at this, but the miscreant was already riding off.

Tucker put his guns away, uttering a curse under his breath, unhitched his own horse, jumped on her back with an ease that spoke of long practice at this kind of art, and chased after the criminal. The man known as Wishart did not seem to have any particular plan for escape, but simply rode through the town at a pace that seemed to augur either a broken neck for him or his pursuer. It was lucky the streets of the town were wide – they had been made that way deliberately for reasons of commerce and cattle drives, or he would have collided with other horses, people and carriages many times. Still, in some cases, he came within a hair's breadth of hitting some hapless passer-by who just happened to be crossing the road.

Tucker took out one of his guns and took aim at the man, holding onto the reins with the other and spurring his horse forward. There was only one problem with doing this: if he had a fault – one that he was ready to admit – he was not the best horseman in the world, and this meant that he had to concentrate a great deal on not actually falling off his steed. He took a shot at the man's retreating back, but predictably this missed Wishart by inches.

They were riding at such a rapid pace that they were getting towards the limits of the town along Silver Street, where the well-kept road within town turned into a bumpy, dusty trail frequented by the miners who worked out in the Mimbres plain beyond the town.

It struck the sheriff that the criminal would have an extensive knowledge of the mines around here – he would make it his business to do so – and that was when he realized what was going on. The gang leader was going to try and hide in the ground and make the sheriff work for his money. At the thought of this, Tucker spurred his horse on.

'Come on, girl,' he said between gritted teeth. 'Extra oats and molasses for you tonight.' The mare, giving her due praise, seemed to respond to this. There was another advantage, in that Wishart was not really dressed for riding and was on an unfamiliar horse. The gelding, which had responded with his flight instinct to the first arrival of the unfamiliar human, did not like the uneven terrain outside town and slowed down in response. It wasn't too long before the two animals were neck and neck.

Tucker had stuck his gun away, and vented his anger in heartfelt shouts that were aimed plainly at the other man.

'Woah,' he shouted. 'Woah, you're not thinking straight, Kurt.' Tucker knew horses well enough to know that they were excited and would ignore any exhortations to stop, but he hoped his words would have an effect on the man, and neither of the animals slowed down. The man known as Wishart cursed loudly at this. He struggled to take the gun from his belt. Tucker coolly assessed the distance between the two animals, pushed his body upwards using the stirrups to take his weight, swayed over to one side and threw his body over the intervening distance.

The weight of the two men was too much and they came off the gelding together and thumped to the ground. It was a jarring fall that took the breath out of both men, a cloud of alkali dust arising around them as they lay there. The horses stopped a short distance from where their riders had fallen and watched what transpired with a degree of academic interest.

After a few seconds the two men staggered to their feet. Wishart reached for his gun, but Tucker pulled back and drew his own weapons, not with quite the ease he had shown before since he had been badly jarred by the fall, but well enough to outgun his opponent. The miscreant turned and started to run, stumbling over the rocks.

'Come on, Kurt, it's over,' he said. But the man who had been known as Wishart turned and raised his gun with intent to shoot the sheriff in the heart.

Tucker fired instinctively, using one gun after the other. His opponent spun around as if hit by a giant hand, then fell to the ground and lay on his back, hatless now, face upturned to the merciless sun. Tucker came forward.

'Reinhardt, you took the wrong path,' he said regretfully. 'We was friends once.'

'Spare me,' said Reinhardt-Wishart. 'You got what you wanted.' Then he gave a harsh gurgle and died.

'No,' said Tucker softly, closing the man's eyes. 'No I didn't.'

Tucker stood with the girl as they looked at the grave of the young sheriff. The mound of earth atop his last resting place was still fresh, and flowers lay beside the gravestone marked 'Frank Mars, sheriff of this parish, lost to us doing his duty.' The graveyard was brand new, replacing the old Boot Hill that had been located near the mines, and was a sunny spot with newly planted trees and well-tended grassy areas, and a red wall all around.

'It was a personal quarrel,' said Tucker. 'You see, Jarrett wanted to go further and do worse in his money extortion,

158

and Frank, who had got himself into something that was way over his head, wanted to pull back. Without consulting his boss, Jarrett took matters into his own hands, thinking the deputies would take over, and not knowing about my arrival.'

'Poor Frank,' said Kathy, 'he just wanted more money because we were going to marry.'

'Well, he didn't go about getting it the right way,' said Tucker.

'I'm sorry he was killed,' said Kathy, 'but imagine if we had married. He would have had all those terrible things hanging over him, and the corruption would have ended it all eventually – our love, I mean.' She hung her head, 'I'm sorry, that sounds awful.'

'Well, Jarrett's going to hang for what he did. The other two . . . Montero was coerced; he's a young boy, I see some hope in him, and I'll make sure his sentence is commuted. As for Hardin, he'll probably get many years in prison.'

'Thanks for all you've done,' said the girl, lifting her head and looking at him with tear-stained cheeks. 'What are you going to do now?'

'Me? I'm going to retire from being a sheriff and take up ranching,' said Tucker, but he caught his breath as the girl seemed to look deep into him with those soft blue eyes. 'Of course you're grieving now, ma'am, but say a man was to sell his interests near Silver City, bring his people over and come and live in a promising part of the world. . . . Could you see your way perhaps to socialising with him and getting to know him better?'

'I like your honesty,' said the girl. 'I have to mourn Frank and what could have been. But yes, I would like to

159

know you better, Mr Tucker.'

'Call me Dan,' he said.

The two of them walked out of the graveyard together, each busy with their own thoughts, but the girl did not protest when he put his arm around her shoulders as they walked towards the carriage that would take them into town.